Chorus of the ALMOST DAMNED

Arsalan

Copyright ©2019 Arsalan

NARRATIVE: AN ADELAIDE-BASED teenager choir wins an Australia-wide competition and gains sufficient funds to participate in the chorals to be staged aChhannakkale/ Gallipoli in April 2015, centenaryof that historic battle. One corporate sponsor, in particular, is enamoured by their very mix, Australian- descended, Kurdish, Armenian and Turkish/ Turkic, which happened by coincidence as much as by design.

His biological grandfather was Armenian, one of the very few children to survive the genocide which coincided with that very battle; he was adopted by a local Turkish family.

That sponsor, Kemal, created an implacable enemy among his relatives during a business trip who found a diabolical way to get even, besides being entirely opposed to any reconciliation between Turks, Kurds and Armenians.

This distant cousin denounces the choir and its members immediately on their arrival in Istanbul, as supporters of Kurdish and Armenian militiae, set up to protect kinsmen in Northern Syria; all kinds of suspicions among Turkish police and military intelligence add to their already- existing prejudices.

A complicating but, at the same time, redeeming, feature, is the fraught relationship that develops between the Armenian- Australian choir-mistress, Arsineh, and Kerem, part of the police detail that keeps her and the choir in limbo.

The teenagers themselves attempt to transcend traditional enmities, yet have to contend with those who threaten to reinforce these.

The Australian consulate, scared by anything that smacks remotely of subversive Mideast teenage militancy, is as unhelpful as it can possibly be, ready to consider the choir and every member actively guilty, not only so as not to offend the Turks, but because it appears too risk- laden and career- damaging to actively help them.

Eventually, Graham, himself an AFP police officer stationed in Istanbul and a music- lover, finds a Jewish musician with the clout to allow the choir to continue practicing in small groups, while he and Kerem eventually succeed to get to the bottom of things, wading through accusations and unspoken suspicions to discover the cause and disentangle the motives of the actual perpetrator.

They realise it is not enough to prove the choir's innocence of any involvement with, or support for, any fighting in Syria, someone has to, in effect, unmask and immobilize his intentions.

Kemal finds out about his choir's predicament and discovers his adoptive relative's motives.

The choir makes it to Chanukkale, with minutes to spare, in spite of vehicle breakdowns, and moves the audience with a triumphant medley of Armenian, Turkish, Kurdish and Australian hymns and songs.

∾

George Mc Manus' introduction to the Levantine Choir of South Australia at the Chanukkalle Centenary:

"In this modern nation of Turkey which has its roots here, we enjoyed the series called the Magnificent Century, celebrating the life and times of her outstanding ruler Suleiman and his remarkable wife Roxanna and the great epoch and empire that they were in charge of; it is my pleasure and great privilege to introduce to you the young voices of a nation which also found its beginnings here, at Chanukkalle, harmonies also of the Empire which have found a home in that young nation of ours, Australia, having left your world but now returning to you in song.

We shall also hear the words of reconciliation by the Father of this modern nation, assuring the mothers of Australia that her sons had now found a home in your soil, along with the sons of the empire and of this nation. Let all the voices, and all the songs, therefore, come home and be reconciled to each other !" spoken in both Turkish and English.

Mustafa Kemal Pasha (Kemal Ataturk)'s words, spoken at the twentieth anniversary of the beginning of WWI:

"Mothers of Australia, rest in peace, assured that your sons have found a home in our soil and that our mothers whose sons likewise rest in this our soil are now likewise the mothers of your sons as well; Mehmet and Johnny, are now brothers and at home forever Mothers of Australia, know therefore: your sons are at peace !

> mothers of the sons who nearby died know now that their souls at rest;
> at peace and well at home, abide, their presence on our soil be blest !
> for the time is truly gone when we of you lived in great fear;
> for as on night follows the Sun, leaves no darkness, makes it clear:

The Creator, only one, gave us splendour, strength and might; in those days, one by one, all we knew was how to fight.
Now we see, deep in our souls, no one lives and dies alone:
For this ground will make us whole; for our nations, this is Home !"

∞

Kerem and Graham first met each other at a sports carnival at Istanbul International School. Both were chaperoning a lady and her boys, Kerem his American- born sister-in-law, while Graham did the honours to a colleague's wife whose husband had gone to attend a funeral in Perth.

Elaine knew Suleikha from previous parent-teacher meetings and introduced Graham to Kerem and her.

"you are with the Australian Federal Police, Graham?" queried Kerem in clear, only slightly accented English while the ladies were distracted;

"working on what, if I may ask?"

"let us get a doner and some tea," said Graham,"and I'll tell you, You a police officer yourself, Kerem?" The Turk nodded.

The men sat down in full view of the boys and girls going through their respective events which created enough noise for the men not to be overheard.

"I work in intelligence, drugs, people smuggling…" Graham stared; for ..

"so do I, on behalf of the Australian government. How come ..?"

"How come? "echoed the Turkish police officer. "I am not very senior, rank of inspector- equivalent; most of what I do is not particularly secret.."

"endangered, are you?"

"not normally," reflected the Turk.

"Married?"

"no, the right one has yet to find me," was the artless reply.

Graham laughed.

"I do consular security, most of the time," he admitted, "a twin role if you like, due to funding cuts… I have yet to be introduced to most of your senior colleagues…."

"been here long, Graham?"

"three months, Kerem; and I have, so far, not been involved in any investigation…"

Kerem clearly did not know where and how to begin:

"You probably know about the youth choir whom we had to put incommunicado on arrival.."

"yes, but I am not officially involved, Kerem; anything particular you would like to know…"

"some feedback from your consulate?"

"why? "astonished,

"because of a comment my colleague made who had first interrogated the teenagers, and their choir mistress…"

"before they even had access to one of ours.. ."

"yes, and I am very sorry; that should not have happened…they are …"

"considered a security risk, Kerem; so I was told," Graham affirmed; "may I mention you when I ask around?"

"no, say, one of your sources; there is something that my colleague noticed and that gives us pause.."

∞

The choir could not have chosen a worse day for arriving in Istanbul; massive demonstration shook the city on legislation that enabled, some said required, the police to use firearms in all situations, including protest; airport intelligence had been told to intercept the choir as soon as it arrived.

"whatever for?" enquired Mehmet Gosel, the section chief. "Young people and a few adults getting readyto sing at Chanukkale in just over a week…."

"these are young Kurds and Armenians who want to join militias to fight ISIS in Northeast Syria.."

"how do we know that?" the intelligence officer wondered.

"Ask not too many questions or you may not like our answers," was the scarcely veiled threat. "We have information to that effect, some of it directly from Adelaide in Australia where they are from."

∞

Kemal's grandfather had been born virtually exactly a hundred years before, at the time of the start of battle at Chanukkalle/ Gallipoli, a few days before the massacre began. The couple, moderately wealthy rug dealers, had hired a wet nurse, a young woman originally from Salonika whose family had left that city, Kemal Ataturk's birthplace, several years ago, after yet another lost war. She had lost her own baby due to typhus; she had plenty of milk and needed the work, so did baby Nerses' natural mother who had to help run the business; except that it never came to that.

The girl had taken the baby to a park, there to breastfeed it, to get out of the house, when the death squads arrived, killing those who resisted or who they had not been specifically ordered to detain. The girl took the baby home, happy to be a mother once again and determined to live down her husband's apprehensions, those of her family and friends. Hamid - his Turkish name- grew up in wartime Istanbul, initially with a lot of Greek friends until they, too, largely disappeared after Mustafa Kemal Pasha's victory in the Twenties; his adoptive mother and family being fluent in that language, from their time in Thrace.

Hamid became a works foreman, proving to be skilled with the new- fangled automobiles to which Turks took with some delight in the interwar years. As his workshop was acquired by a General Motors subsidiary in the, quite bleak, Fifties, he was facing a choice: migrate to Europe or Australia. Since he had picked up some English from his new bosses, he took his family, the result of an arranged marriage, to Perth, there to work at the Holden plant.

Enver, his second-oldest son, trained as a welder and moved to Adelaide with his then- girlfriend, daughter of a Mildura grape farmer, when Mitsubishi opened its plant in that city. When he had saved enough money, he had his grandmother, the girl originally from Salonika, now Thessaloniki, visit him at his very convenient home in Goodwood, walking distance to the factory. Enver's wife, the grape grower's daughter, took the ancient Thracian lady to as many places in the region as she could think of, including the Riverland and Mildura, there for her to meet her own parents.

It was on the long drive back to Adelaide that the matriarch spoke:

"I used to work for an Armenian family once…."

"when, Nana?" the young woman asked politely.

"In the early years of World War One."

"was that not when they all got killed, Nana?"

"how do you know, daughter? Nobody in Turkey ever talks about that.."

"we do, in Australia; it was mentioned in school and two of the little ones at nursery are Armenian- Australian..", referring to her son's daycare centre that she relied on to be able to work part- time.

"we are not even allowed, by law, to talk about it in Turkey, certainly not to call it a massacre. We are told that Armenians had formed militias to help the enemy.."

"did the family that you had worked for belong to one of these," wondered the girl, now interested.

"None of them were; they were good people and very good employers."

The old lady made up her mind.

"We passed this Armenian church a few days ago…"

"oh, on our way out through the northern suburbs; lovely singing.."

"which I had not heard since.. must have been over sixty years ago; I was nineteen and had lost a child born earlier that year and the family hired me as a wet- nurse and child minder; we were refugees from what is now inside Greece and needed the money; there was a church of theirs at the end of the road; it is not in use.."

"never ever since?"

"yes, daughter. On the day that they came.."

"came to kill your Armenian employers.. "

"well, they were detained; for the government waited if someone were to ransom them.."

"like a cousin in the United States, you mean..?"

"or some well.- known people in the wider world; there was this composer- Komitas- who was rescued and ended up in Paris. Anyway, I was told that the entire family died in detention, as did thousands in that neighbourhood alone. Except.."

Her granddaughter-in-law listened intently. "you must have a reason for telling me, Nana."

"yes, I do; the people, mainly my own family, in Istanbul who knew are now dead; that's my own parents, God bless them, my brothers, another sister; we never told anyone else…"

"told them what, Nana?" all ear now.

"that your father-in-law started life as an Armenian baby. They came early in the morning, first light, but I had already gone out with little Nerses- his name in those days- through a back lane to get some bread and nurse him at the same time as he had not given his mother any sleep. As soon as I heard shots, screaming, the works, I kept moving till I got home, without even thinking about what to do next. It was my own mother.. excuse me," the old lady cried, overcome by memories. "my baby had been her first grandson you know, and she had missed it more than I did, at the time; I was young and knew I would have more. It persuaded me.."

"the way your mum responded, you mean?" demanded the young woman.

"yes, I decided to keep him; we got the local Imam to issue a naming document- my baby had died too soon for that, and not many people knew at the time that Nerses was a substitute for young dead baby Hamid.."

"so he became Hamid."

"and grew up as such, learning a modern trade, had a family, migrated on the strength of a welder's ticket and some English, rather than go to Germany as most men did, and still do."

"why are you telling me all this, Nana?" asked the grape grower's daughter, mother of toddler Kemal.

"For one thing, the singing brought it on," the old lady explained. "I grew up at a time and in a place where we lived together as good neighbours, Greeks, Turks, Macedons, Armenians, Bulgarians, Jews even; it hasn't happened in Turkey since."

"nor will it?" Kemal's mother wondered.

"Probably not," her grandmother- in-law replied, "but I can see it happening here in a very strange way, Australia has inherited the people if not the customs of our old Empire, something that is beginning to be important again in Turkey, except we cannot recover it. I hope the young people here can; which is, perhaps, why I told you…."

"so young Kemal's grandfather was born an Armenian, baby Nerses?"

The two women were quiet on their way back to Goodwood.

∞

There was no doubt that Arsineh was a genuine recognized Armenian herself, albeit in the third generation. There had never been a doubt in her or her parents' minds that she would end up at the Conservatory; she had been singing Armenian songs in and out of church ever since she was a very little child but she also displayed an eclectic taste in music, being a competent keyboard and xylophone player and a mean hand with the Tar as well; she did Blues, Country& Western, as well as classical music; yet her great love was for contemporary Levantine and Iranian music. Her mentor encouraged her to train as a composer and conductor; no better place than the South Australian Conservatory.

She soon specialized on youth choirs and orchestras, partly because she was not much older than many of her students but mainly because she was very good at it; never too strict for the sake of strictness but meticulous almost to a fault, a rare contradiction, in Arsineh's case, it worked,

As can be imagined, she was passionate about everything and everyone she cared about. She had taken up with a married flautist, not least because any sound that he was unable to extract from his instrument would not otherwise exist, even in one's imagination; she had felt something special whenever she conducted him along with her singers; she coaxed an even more remarkable achievement out of Brendan, as well as out of her singers, each time it happened, even during rehearsals.

The applause had been thunderous at their concert, at Elders Hall, fesaturing a chamber orchestra and selected singers of hers. He had reacted to her conducting by anticipating her every move and produced a sound which inspired the rest of the orchestra and her singers alike; no wonder they sparked off each other in bed, each time they had a chance.

Arsineh had had boyfriends, at school, at the conservatory, had even answered an ad once. Strangely enough, the thing she liked most about Brendan was that he never demeaned his wife to his lover but would mention her as someone who he was genuinely fond of and whose strengths and weaknesses he understood well. He was highly realistic about himself, with a sense of wry humour.

The full choir and orchestra had cut a record somewhat over a year ago, with an outstanding contribution by Brendan, surpassed only by Samira, a Palestinian-descended girl soloist, and Arsineh's conducting. They had made love almost immediately afterwards, feeling the sheer force and perfection of their passion for each other   It was partly on the strength of that record that Brendan had been offered a scholarship at the Juillard in New York, along with the percussionist and the violone (bass) player, an ethnic Greek. Their parting was painful; for Brendan felt compelled to take Monique, his young wife, along who very much wanted to study photography at de Niro's studio.

It was to help herself manage her grief which she could, obviously, not admit to anyone that the girl had thrown herself into getting her youth choir ready for competitive selection for the Gallipoli centenary.

The person who had drawn her attention to a newspaper feature was none other than Brendan's brother, a music teacher, aware of Arsineh's misery.

"I had a look at the Advertiser's weekend cultural pages, Arsi..", he rang her one evening.

"Do you read them at all," he asked his brother's lost lover.

"I normally do," she admitted," but I was too busy cleaning out every copy that was not an original score.."

"oh, a visit by the copyright people, I see," her friend surmised.

"Yes, we had a tip-off that APRA would visit us on Monday.."

"and the penalties for unauthorized copies can be very steep.."

"enough to put our choir out of business; it has happened to others; what were you trying to tell me, George?"

"Well, find the paper in the Library, Arsi; but anyway, there is a competition for the centenary concert to be held at Chanukkalle…"

"where's that?"

"along the Dardanelles, southwest of Istanbul, Galubulu in Turkish…"

"oh, the Gallipoli centenary in April. A competition, George?"

"yes, in stages, it seems, states, then region, then all- Australian…"

"age-specific as well?"

"I think so, Arsi."

∞

The girl found, to her surprised delight, that ethnic teenage choirs were to occupy an inside track in the forthcoming series of ascending competitions; yet she decided to first get stuck into fundraising, partly because they needed money but mainly to focus on the campaign; for that was what the series of singing contests was. She timed a forthcoming Eisteddfod in the Riverland, northeast of Adelaide, as a massive rehearsal, not only for fundraising and parental awareness, but also to trim her team and develop and practice the kind of music they wanted to perform at Gallipoli a few months hence. Doing something that both of them would have liked helped dull the pain of Brendan's departure.

She had her charges discover both traditional and modern Levantine music, Kurdish, Turkish, Armenian, Georgian, Arab and Aramean/ Assyrian; she also made a study of Komitas, a last-century Armenian musicologist credited with refining and rescuing Armenian music. Not that she was against fusion:

"as long as it fits into some sort of Levantine template.."

"Like the original Turkish empire?" Brendan's brother queried.

"Yes, let us bring back to Turkey the voices that she lost this last century.." she replied while looking at her departed lover's brother, barely able to stop herself from bawling out loud.

∞

As many as fifteen choirs had competed in the Renmark Rose Festival

Eistedfodd, and it took a fully flawless performance by Arsineh's Teen Levantines to barely edge past the entire competition; as a bonus, she managed a full night's sleep for the first time since Brendan's departure at the caravan park where the choir had bunked up, waking up with a smile; for she had dreamt of having been made the most passionate love to.

"My greatest difficulty is that I have to train and get ready a few extra boys and girls from each community, surplus to the number we will be able to take to Turkey but necessary," she explained to a girl friend over coffee on East Terrace one evening, after a particularly strenuous but rewarding rehearsal, with melodies of all kind swirling in her head.

"why, Arsi?" the other girl wondered, looking at her sexy friend.

"because there'll always be girls and boys who miss out, for family reasons, school exams, sports or illness…"

"almost like a sports team.." her friend surmised.

" Yes, and those who miss out will be most upset, as will their parents…"

"then you'll have to remind your kids and their parents time and time again that it is so," commented the other girl. Arsineh nodded, once again reminded of Brendan's type of commonsense advice.

∞

Kerem and Graham met near the Topkapi for a glass of tea; Graham had bought some Ekmek (loaf of bread) at the government shop and heartily bit into it while sipping his tea.

"We are no longer allowed to investigate with any degree of independence anything that involves protests, disruption of traffic or disturbance of the peace, let alone the merest whiff of terrorist, but treat it as proven and something to be controlled.."

"even if not true?"

"especially if it is not true and also, regardless of who or what may have caused it; that, in particular, is something we may no longer ask ourselves.."

"your prosecutors likewise?"

"yes, Graham; very recent legislation has taken away their ability of independent investigation, same as ours, of anything that disturbs 'national equilibrium '…"

"and who defines 'national equilibrium', Kerem?"

"guess who…"

"our team at the consulate is likewise paralysed at the thought of getting involved with anything that smacks of 'terrorists; 'we try neither to upset public opinion in Australia nor your government in this country …"

"even at the expense of your young people who may well be innocent.."

"were it not for their parents," Graham commented, "nobody would allow them be not guilty as charged, neither here nor back home.." rather bitterly.

"Don't say that," replied the Turk. "One of my colleagues…"

"who had interrogated them?"

"yes, he had been with the original team who intercepted them at the airport; he keeps saying.."

∞

The choir found itself whisked away straight from the aircraft that had brought them from Dubai, rather than going through passport control and customs, confused after a series of long, crowded flights and very tired.

Two women police officers separated Arsineh from her charges, handcuffed and led her in to a windowless interrogation room. She had to wait hours, barely suppressing her urge to pee; eventually, having banged at the door numerous times, she was led to a reasonably clean toilet, in full view of the airport police station.

For some reason, she would not say anything, even refuse the customary cup of tea, except to demand consular assistance. Eventually, a consular officer appeared, evidently unhappy with his role and presence:

"why am I here and what has happened to my choir?"

"if you do not know,"the diplomat replied,"do you expect me to tell you?"

"yes, Sir," the young woman replied, spiritedly, even though she had not eaten, drunk or slept since her arrest.

"you will find out," the man assured her.

" How about my choir and how about rehearsals? Aren't you aware that we are to represent Australia at Chanukkalle?"

"what is that?"

"the Turkish name for Gallipoli; I would have thought that you knew that; you live in Istanbul, don't you?"

"yes; what do you want your choir to rehearse for; you will not be allowed to perform; we'll be lucky if we can persuade the Turks to allow you and the choir to return to Australia. We'll have to promise to prosecute you back home and none of you'll ever get a passport again."

Arsineh struggled to think through this accusation, in spite of her extreme distress and fatigue:

"You can't mean that we are terrorists, Sir?"

"terrorist sympathizers.."

"says who?"

"say Turkish Intelligence and that is good enough for us; you know what legislation is like back home, ever since the IslamicState…"

"are we, any of us, accused of sympathise with the Da'esh.."

"who are they?"

"are you a diplomat who lives and works in this region?" she omitted 'Sir' by now.

"Yes, what's that got to do with it?"

"Da'esh is shorthand for the Islamic State?"

"How do you know all this if you are no sympathizer?" the consul asked.

"We read the papers; but if it is not the Islamic State, who is my choir to be in sympathy of? We only have six young Arabs among us, and half of us aren't even Muslim, nor am I."

"I don't know," the diplomat admitted, "nor do I care; the Turks do have to cope with all kinds of militias; you should know that if you say you prepared yourself and your choir, you say?"

"I have nothing to say to you, Sir, other than remind you and your colleagues that we are entitled to every bit of assistance.."

"not as terrorist sympathizers, you are not.," decided the consul and left.

An obviously senior policeman entered who must have overheard the conversation.

"Do you need anything?" he enquired.

"yes, space so that we can rehearse," Arsineh replied instantly.

"we are a choir and not a bunch of terrorists…"

"but you are Armenians. Kurds and Arabs.."

"generations away from this region; everyone in my choir is the son or daughter of people who were also born in Australia, myself included; we are the Levantine Singers, known as the Voice of the Levant !"

"it appears not, but I'll see if you' ll be allowed to rehearse, and where. How about notes?"

"I do not know what to tell you, Sir."

"then, tell me nothing, Miss; I see what can be done…"

∽

Fered Inonu, that was his name, left the interrogation room deep in thought. His opinion of Australian consuls was not very exalted, based on previous experience, both with known criminals as with those unfortunate enough to have been attacked or stuff stolen, common in any big city. The diplomat's refusal to even listen, let alone stand up for his young compatriots and their minder, rated him so contemptible as Fered Inonu could scarcely imagine himself to be capable of.

"the thing that impressed me most was the girl's insistence not on freedom, or even on an explanation," he had explained to Kerem, retelling the scene,

"but on being able to rehearse with her choir."

"From the little that I know about musicians," agreed Graham, "that would be their number one priority. Why did the girl not answer when your colleague asked her about notes?"

"she must have remembered that there were Kurdish and Armenian songs among them.."

"which you are not allowed to sing in public," remembered Graham.

"we had a parliamentarian arrested some years back, for speaking Kurdish in Parliament; what got into them for wanting to sing such songs at Chanukalle?"

"The voice of a lost empire," stated Graham, intuitively.

"Fered was also saying this: 'the girl was right not to say anything further; for even if we find out what really happened and even if we can prove their innocence, we, the police, will not be allowed to stop prosecuting them, nor will the prosecutors ..'"

"who can, Kerem?"

"the government, as a concession to yours, Graham," replied the policeman, thoughtfully.

"That would need a lot more engagement than we have seen the consulate capable of, so far," agreed Graham.

"How about parents?"

"yes, some pressure is building up," commented Graham, "which the department of foreign affairs has sat on so far, with threats of invoking anti-terrorist legislation…"

"Is everyone gone mad?" exclaimed Kerem. People in the café were turning their heads in astonishment.

"Someone may have to work out, in Australia, what really happened and then put pressure on your government, along with every single parent, friend and relative…"

"what can we do here, Kerem?"

"identify an unimpeachable music lover to help these young people rehearse…"

"anyone you have in mind, Kerem?"

"yes, I may need help, though.."

Sixteen-year old Birke, an alto voice, would have, among the Levantine Singers, been the one best prepared for surprises, such as arbitrary arrests and detention; for she had been in Istanbul during the Taksin Square agitation when the citizens of Istanbul had demonstrated, initially to save the last open space in their city; it had degenerated into a display of general unhappiness; several of her cousins had been arrested for at least a few days and even more been manhandled; she and her mother had narrowly avoided being detained several days later and nowhere even near Taksin Square.

"If anything like that happens while you are in Turkey.."

"why should it, Mum?" asked the girl over a cup of tea while they were sitting on their veranda, preparing some eggplant for dinner.

"you never know;" her mother replied;

"look, we Turks are the salt of the earth and the most generous people alive, but like salt…"

"too much of a good thing .."

"yes, anyway, claim Australian citizenship, demand to be put in touch with the consulate, and use your judgment whether to speak Turkish or not. Otherwise, say nothing, whatever they charge you with.."

Her brother changed her SIM card over to a universal one that she could use anywhere, instructing her to ring him at the slightest hint of trouble.

When police at SagriheGogchen Airport started herding this group of wildly protesting, totally bewildered teenagers, Bilke manoeuvred herself close to a few girls and mouthed 'toilet'; as soon as they got inside the building, they refused to move, quick-witted and uncommunicative as teenagers can be sometimes:

"Peepee," Birke shrilled across the corridor, and the other girls chorused an immediate, quite genuinely need to go to the toilet, as they had not been allowed to for almost forty minutes before touchdown because of turbulence above the Aegean. Eventually, two policewomen herded the girls into an airport toilet.

"Block the door and make a lot of noise,"

Bilke instructed her friends, then carefully extricated her mobile, hoping not to be noticed. Two Armenian girls, fellow alto voices, stood in front of her toilet door, calling for her to hurry up but also preventing the policewomen from getting any closer.

Her brother's answerphone kicked in, in Turkish and English; she left a quick message in Turkish:

"we are being arrested at SagriheGogchen Airport; I do not know what for; ask Mum to ring back.." which she repeated twice.

Birke's mother, a nurse, had been on night shift and was dead-tired when she got home but wide awake when her son ran his sister's message past her. She managed to get hold of Mara of the Multicultural Centre Street at her home.

"I'll ring a contact of mine in Canberra; do you know anyone at the Australian consulate in Istanbul?" her friend asked Birke's mother.

"yes, but he is back in Australia; let me give you his number.. could you also ring a few journalists whether they know of anything going on in Turkey..".

" yes, I have those contacts," the multicultural lady replied; "I'll have to ring them later, what with time difference. I'll do the Advertiser and the Department of Foreign Affairs in an hour or so; they'll be at work by then; you have just come off work, haven't you?"

"yes," confirmed Birke's mother, "and I need to get some sleep, otherwise I'll be of no use on shift tonight."

"take some sleeping tablets," advised her friend, "but before you do, see if you can ring your daughter.."

"if she can answer her phone or whether it has been confiscated,"

Birke's mother understood, knowing the methods of the Turkish police force.

"I'll do that and then I'll ring you straightaway.."

"do that, but then let me do all this other phoning; we are Multicultural Affairs and a lot better equipped to deal with those things.."

Birke's mum lost no time; her daughter's telephone had not been switched off but the person who picked it up after the third ring did not introduce herself :

"stop this conversation straightaway.." in Turkish;

"why?"

"you are not allowed to ask that question," the policewoman's voice answered; "where are you ringing from?"

"Australia; where else; I am Birke's mother.." also in Turkish; "how dare you not tell me what you have dome to my daughter and her friends; they are the official Australian choir…"

"take it up with your government, then," the policewoman commented and hung up, turning off Birke's mobile in the process.

Birke's mum replayed the conversation to her friend:

"that must be some anti-terrorist police force," the ladies agreed, "but whatever for?"

"I do not know but if we are right," the multicultural lady asserted," then we'll have difficulty with our own government; they won't want to do anything.."

"ring them nonetheless, please.."

Which she did; the person she got hold of on the twenty- four hotline had been sympathetic but unable to help.

"I'll get your contact to get in touch with you," she promised; "we have nothing on our screen on Australia's official teenage choir, you said; why is the mother not ringing us? "

"because Birke's mother works shifts at the Royal Adelaide; I persuaded her that we at Multicultural Affairs are better set up than she as an individual.."

Mara then rang the community editor at the Advertiser who, too, was unaware of anyone, let alone a teenage choir, having been arrested in Istanbul:

"Look, I have contacts in Istanbul, people I meet at conferences or on assignments; use your own contacts also. A word to the wise; don't expect much from the people in Canberra.."

"how about the consulate in Istanbul?"

"call them PWB…People without Backbone !"

After a while, her friend at the Advertiser rang back.

"We tried Canberra, same as you did; they know nothing so far; if it has anything to do with terrorism.."

"why should it?"

"why, indeed; yet if that was the conclusion that you and your friend, the girl's mother, reached, when she tried to reach her daughter and got hold of that policewoman, instead; the department will be very reluctant to find out what really happened and what to do about it."

"Have you got better news, all the same? "the culture lady asked.

"Yes, I rang my contacts, bit difficult, what with time difference; one of them told me that a colleague of his had witnessed their arrest and had told the editor; expect a call from him in a few hours."

The one who called first was her Canberra contact, instead.

"Would you tell me exactly what you know, Mara; why is the mother not ringing us?"

"because she is asleep, having been on shift; she then has a family to organize before she goes back to work; apart from which, this is an Adelaide-based choir and you'll get other parents to ring you soon. The young ones are held incommunicado…."

"oh, that does not sound good; how do you know?"

"before I tell you, have you heard from the consulate in Istanbul?"

"not that I know… let me ring you back…"

She remembered a series of articles in the Advertiser about the various competitions involving the Voices of the Levant with their songs and singers from various cultures, she had kept the papers; so she decided to consult them in the hope of finding a local contact. Meanwhile, it was time for her tea break.

A colleague saw her with the papers:

"what are you looking for, Mara?"

"a local contact for the Voices of the Levant."

"aren't they the teenage choir who is to represent us at Gallipoli this April?"

"yes, it turns out they were summarily detained on arrival in Istanbul."

"My daughter's music teacher knows the conductor.."

"how come?"

"one day, he brought a record along featuring their conductor and his own brother, a flautist. Let me see whether I can ring him…."

As the ladies were finishing their tea, her colleague helped her carry the papers into their office.

"Mr McManus, that's my daughter's teacher, will ring you in a few minutes; the lady at his school wanted to know why, at first. "

"what did you tell her?"

"we needed local contact from the Voices of the Levant, and he was the only one I could think of, through his brother's link to their conductor."

∽

That was what was on Brendan's brother's mind upon ringing back:

"you need a link to the young lady who conducted Brendan's award-winning record, do you?"

"yes, we understand she is in charge of the Singers of the Levant who represent Australia for their age group."

"they should have just arrived in Istanbul; anything happen to them?"

"yes, we are afraid."

"it is strange; it was I who suggested to Arsineh…"

"the conductress.."

"yes, a very young one, Arsineh Gergoriyan…"

"Armenian? "

"as you know, half their choir is; anyway, after Brendan left it was I who suggested that she get her choir to compete to perform in their age slot at Gallipoli…"

"quite a convoluted process it proved to be.."

"o yes; what do you think happened?" She told him.

"if they are held on suspicion of abetting any sort of regional terrorism, whether 'tis true or not, I don't hold out much hope of the department wanting to get involved," the music teacher's brogue was ever more pronounced,

"must be the Irish in me and me brother. Tell you what; I'll let me brother know.."

"you said he'd left; where?"

"The Juillard in New York, on the strength of the record that your colleague remembered. I'll let him know…"

18 • Chorus of the Almost Damned

"any particular reason?"

"yes, Arsineh has been missing him ever so much since which is why I suggested that she and her singers compete; so I do feel responsible as well; Brendan might have a few contacts, besides."

∞

Mara found the emergency hotline for the Australian consulate in Istanbul among her computer files, as distinct from the one in Canberra; they had needed it when her own niece had been trapped in the Izmit earthquake some years ago.

"Australian consulate in Istanbul, emergency service, Lester Bean speaking…"

Mara explained the situation as she knew it, so far.

"You said that the policewoman who picked up the phone said no one was allowed to ring that phone…it has a Turkish SIM, how come?"

"the girl's brother had fitted an international one before she left Adelaide with her choir…"

"what are they called?"

"Levantine Singers/ the Voices of the Levant, Sir."

"Hold the line; I'll try the line myself…"

she could hear him dial a number, say something in Turkish, then go very silent. It took a long time for him to get back:

"did you suspect that the choir is being held on suspicion of aiding and abetting terrorism?"

"since you are asking, yes."

"you ought not to have rung me, or anyone on this number. How did you get hold of it, anyway…"

"to do with the earthquake a few years back. But will you not make representations on behalf of a teenage choir which is to represent Australia at the centenary?"

"we may be able to ensure that they get a fair trial, and I am telling you too much already."

"You mean, Mr Bean, that there may not be a trial at all?"

"my lips are sealed; do not try to contact anyone else at this consulate…"

"the parents will…" the gentleman ended the conversation with an audible sigh.

∾

It is never easy to time it right if you live in Adelaide and your brother in New York. George Mc Manus had to wait till almost ten o' clock at night to get hold of his brother, catching him as he was about to leave for the Juillard at quarter to nine in the morning, US East Coast Time. Brendan listened, then asked:

"I did know that Arsineh's choir had managed; don't ask me how, but let me thank you for suggesting to her to try.." he paused, then asked: "you know more about her fundraising efforts in and around Adelaide than I would, not least because of the distance and time difference involved. Give some thought whether you can identify a key donor or sponsor, then contact him or her; meanwhile, I'll ask some of our resident Turkish musicians what to do in such a situation. We had a few Sephardic musicians here a few month ago…"

"Ladino singers, Brendan?"

"Yes, I seem to remember they were in touch with their mates in Istanbul ."

"we had that Ladino girl here in Adelaide a few years back; her father was himself a Sephardic singer and composer, born in Istanbul…"

"can you identify and motivate Arsineh's prime mover? Try …"

"you miss her, don't you?"

"you bet."

Brendan braced himself for a difficult admission to his wife Monique, a New Caledonian- born budding photographer with ambitions to work for a big news agency.

"You realize that I have to help her and the young people in her choir, don't you?" while she remained silent.

"Let me give you one reason for you to listen to before you consider divorcing me," he pleaded.

"and that would be?" his wife demanded, in spite of herself.

"That I'd do exactly the same for you if.."

"if what, Brendan?"

"you want to become an international professional photographer; don't think that you won't be at risk.."

"being at the wrong place at the wrong time, seeing the wrong thing, talking to the wrong people, you mean?"

"yes, if you are anywhere near good in your work, that is bound to happen;

and I shall go to the same length to help you out, whether you divorce me or not, as I am about to, for a girl whom I did love very much…"

Monique's Gallic temperament was in visible conflict with the innate pragmatism of her race:

"look, give me some space; for I shall need a few nights and days to think through what this means to us.."

"us?"

"yes, us, even though you are about to help your ex-lover…"

"and a choir full of teenagers who will have to live under that accusation for I don't know how long."

His wife nodded, slapped, then kissed him and left the house, sobbing.

∾

Brendan decided, rather than mope, to start by contacting his supervisor, the Dean, as well as his Turkish colleagues.

The musicologist, a specialist in wind instruments, listened quietly, carefully, then stared out of his office window for several minutes:

"did you tell your wife, Brendan?"

"yes, almost as soon as my brother had told me."

"would you rather not wait until you know more?"

"by that time, it may be too late. If my brother was wrong or rather those who told him, I shall owe an apology to any number of people, so will my brother and whoever informed him; but it won't cost my life or livelihood; if my brother was right, then there may be no time to lose…"

"why would that be, Brendan?"

"for one thing, they were only meant to spend one week, ten days max, in Turkey before the Centenary. And as you know, Sir, with terrorism charges, no one wants to investigate the rights or wrongs; instinctive reactions set in."

"you may be right, Brendan; I understand that the present government in Turkey has its own rather less than accommodating ways of dealing with opposition, real or perceived; a choir that insists on singing Kurdish and Armenian songs as well as Turkish ones would be viewed with suspicion. Nonetheless, who would denounce them like that?"

"do you believe that' s what it was?"

"as likely as not, Brendan."

"So does my brother, the music teacher back in Adelaide."

"Did he say that?"

"he asked for possible sponsors, if I knew any, to have an idea who or what the choir…"

"or the sponsor.."

"may have been up against."

"but what is your priority, Brendan?" the musicologist asked.

"To get them permission and space to rehearse."

"I can see how it would help these young people; it would need a very highly respected and entirely uninvolved person, someone above any suspicion, well connected, knowledgeable…I think I know the very person.."

He then told Brendan about Yishak Zwi Levi by his Jewish name:

"calls himself Esak Ebed in Turkish, a well- known instrumentalist and specialist on Levantine music," he explained: "he is one of the few artistes who can play the Ney.."

"that's the Farsi flute.",

"yes, of course, you are a flautist, and the Tar.."

"the single- string Kurdish/Iranian string instrument.."

"simultaneously; he used to be a Ladino singer when he was younger.."

"Sephardic musicality, "commented Brendan, "we had a young Sephardi woman singing her own Ladino compositions in Adelaide some years back whose father, if I remember rightly, was born in Turkey."

"we had Yishak conduct a master class on Levantine instruments here three years ago, and I do meet him from time to time at concerts and conferences."

"does he live in Istanbul and does he have the standing with the Islamist government, for him to intercede…"

"we can but try, Brendan; he may suggest someone even better suited; at the very least, we'll get some background."

"we, Sir?"

"yes, my days of passionate affairs with young Armenian choir mistresses may be well over but I do not like choristers sequestered any more than you, especially teenagers chosen to represent their country."

Brendan had a text message: "forgiven, provisionally and for the time being, provided that I come along to Istanbul to test my photographic skills and nerve 'under fire.'Get time off the Juillard, Brendan, or else…"

∽

Kemal had made a career out of nano-particulate lamination, essential in high-quality three-dimensional printing. He had inherited considerable mechanical skills from his father and grandfather, the welders and carmakers who had made good in Australia, and had been able to study at Adelaide, Berlin and the MIT in Boston, honing his engineering and allowing him access to the newest technological concepts.

Having, eventually, been told by his mother, for his reputed great-grandmother, baby Nerses/ Hamids 'mother' from Salonika had, meanwhile, died, of his hidden Armenian ancestry, he sought opportunities to help any such initiatives as Arsineh's, much as these would have been unpopular if not impossible in Turkey. He visited that country very often, as also Israel and the Middle East where many of his suppliers were based.

He would invariably spend time with his Turkey- based relatives, descended from his father's and grandfather's cousins of whom there had been many.

∽

One such cousin, several rungs removed, was a young businessman called Ismet who, while quite wealthy and well-connected, was secretly jealous of Kemal. While Kemal was as uxorious as the next person, Ismet's marriage was under threat, partly because of his wife's Sara's frustrated ambitions after more than a decade of having been married to him but mainly because of what she interpreted as his indifference to her and to those of no immediate use to him, quite apart from his predilection for his girlfriends, again in contrast to faithful, empathetic and helpful Kemal .

∽

While in the Kurdish region of East Turkey, near Dogubayit, Kemal was directed to a farm coop where rare earth had been discovered.

"The management wants to attract an investor in return for ongoing sales of the refined product," Kemal was told.

"You being a nano-specialist, they would like to know of any industrial application, by itself or in connection with any other process; plus they'd like to know how best to refine it.."

"you need to worry about toxicity, for one thing," Kemal told the resource broker who had made the initial contact. "I can suggest a toxicity testing procedure if you can name a laboratory; plus I can commission a design for its refining process, basically a very highly leak-proof tailings dam and a series of sluices, in return for exclusive delivery at a mutually agreed-on long term price range, allowing for your fees and mine, for service and the strength of my recommendation."

"Have you any use of the material in your own process, Efendi?" the broker asked, using the archaic address.

"I am prepared to buy the entire supply, provided that it can be refined and toxicity- tested to my specifications; you are welcome to your due diligence,"

"you mean, I have to find out myself ," the Kurd commented.

"More or less; who, by the way, will be responsible for compliance; you and your team, or the miners?"

"the farm coop, with my help," was the reply.

∾

It was only a few days later that Ismet got hold of the same Kurdish resource broker; they too, had tea, arak and a good meal. Ismet had been contacted by a German industrialist who wanted that particular rare earth for special paints and to insert into particularly strong polymers. Unknowingly, he went through the same steps with the broker as his distant cousin had done, with one vital exception.

The broker, being an honest man, had already made certain promises to certain local contractors and also contacted a laboratory in Shivas, equipped to deal with the highly toxic material. Over yet another few glasses of arak and endless cups of tea, he told Ismet that the entire supply had been pre- contracted to a Turkish-Australian industrialist.

"No, I shall not tell you who; there aren't too many who have a use for this kind of material."

"what made his offer different from mine?" asked Ismet, genuinely bewildered. "Price? "

"No, fairly similar to what your client was able to offer.."

"what else?" wondered Ismet.

"The other gentleman ensured that all the work that needs to be done.."

"building a retention dam; testing for toxicity; working out an extraction schedule.."

"yes, all these things; but this industrialist was prepared to use local enterprise and institutions, unlike your client who wants to use German consultants, equipment and facilities.."

"which he is prepared to pay for," argued Ismet.

"To be sure, but I am always happy for local people and facilities to get the few jobs that exist around here, as is the farm coop who owns the land and the material. So, they decided to go ahead to honour his offer, not yours, Sir;

I am sure that you have done the right thing by your German client but, there you are; I am very sorry."

∾

Ismet had been in Germany most of the time that Kemal had been in Turkey but he did recognize him from a photo in a back copy of the local newspaper, part of an article on a 'do' by the local chamber of commerce.

To have been done out of a lucrative contract by a cousin, however much removed, was too much, especially since his business had not been doing too well lately; he was also staring at a potentially expensive divorce if some recent comments at home were anything to go by.

Ismet was not of the forgiving kind and kept an eye out for a chance of taking his revenge, as soon as he got back to Istanbul.

Several weeks later, he had tea with an uncle whom he genuinely liked and who had just returned from spending time with their relatives in Perth and Adelaide.

"They are preparing for the centenary at Canukkalle all over Australia," he told his nephew;

"there will be many Europeans, Australians and New Zealanders, more than usual," Ismet agreed. "I work with several touring companies as a capacity broker and I am doing quite well from it all," (he did not mention that this was the only endeavour that had done well for him recently).

"Is any of our relatives involved in any way," he asked, not expecting a specific answer.

"Well, you'll be surprised, Ismet; your cousin Kemal is…"

"he was here while I was away," his nephew said, not betraying any interest.

"yes, he was all over the country, as usual; as soon as he got to Adelaide, someone associated with a choir approached him for help; they needed to win several competitions and travel all over Australia to be allowed to represent their country at Chanakkalle this April.."

"did they manage?"

"from what I remember, they needed to do well in one more competition…"

"did cousin Kemal help out; I know he is very generous."

(he can afford to; he got an entire production of rare earth for a song, Ismet thought)

"Yes, Ismet, not only did Kemal donate, he organized all kinds of people, Greeks, Armenians, Lebanese, even Iraqui Kurds…"

"people who live in Australia, Uncle?"

"descendants of those who once made up our empire, Ismet; what could have been more fitting."

"how about the choir itself, Uncle?"

"teenagers, I met a few at a … gathering," his uncle did not want to admit that it had been at an Assyrian church.

"Same backgrounds as the people that cousin Kemal raised money from, Uncle?"

"yes, Armenians, Jews, Arabs, Turks, a few Anglos…"

"what are they called, Uncle? "

"oh, let me think.. I got it," beamed his uncle: "Levantine Singers/Voices of the Levant."

∽

Brendan's Turkish fellow master students knew Esak Ebed at least by reputation; two offered to ring the old musician personally:

"we don't need to know what you need to contact him for; you are a very good musician and a good person; that is enough for us.." the kind of humaneness he had come to expect from Turks and, truth be told, from people in the Levant generally and music lovers in particular.

Ebed Esak, not well known as Yishak Zwi Levi in his home town of Istanbul, lived in a spacious house near Zirkesi, off the Marmara Sea, his family home for many generations; some claimed that his ancestor had acquired within years of having arrived from Segovia in Spain in the very late fifteenth century, a few years after the final Reconquista, the alternative having been for him and his family to have to convert and spend the rest of their lives as Marranos, exercising a warped form of Judaism in secret which many former Jews had done.

Yishak would often practice on the rooftop, regardless of the weather, and even conduct classes there at times.

He'd get up very early each morning, more or less in time for Iftar, the Islamic early morning prayer, prayed a version of the Kaddish in praise of YHWH to thank the Lord for yet another day, then practiced singing or playing on a choice of instruments; meanwhile, his granddaughters would have breakfast ready before heading off for school; he'd kiss them all, listen to their giggles and excited chatter, then let them loose on the world and retired for a few hours of reading or resting prior to cycling to the studio run by a Sephardic FM station where he taught and recorded, the studio having been funded and set up by a band of his former students who had become a famous pop group, mixing Sephardic, Turkish and general Levantine music.

His former student, and a source of great pride to Yishak, Tereq, waited till midnight, New York time, so as to get hold of the maestro almost as soon as the old artiste got up. He managed to raise one of the grand-daughters, instead, who answered the phone quite sleepily, waking up during the conversation with the student whom she remembered and liked whenever he had visited their home.

"I'll call Efendi," using the respectful but generally forbidden title for elderly gentlemen of standing.

"Tereq, my son," the aged scholar picked up the phone,

"good to hear from you. What is the weather like in the Big Apple," taking great, if innocent, pains at the breadth of his knowledge.

"The Big Apple is a bit sort of asthmatic, Sir, but the weather has been very good, not too hot. How's home?"

"cool in the morning and a bit stifling during the day. I try not to work during the middle of the day.."

"like a Siesta, Sir?"

"more like in an Anatolian village in high summer, son. What time is it now, in New York?" he asked suddenly.

"Almost midnight, Sir?" was the reply.

"In that case, I suspect yours is not a social call, son; tell us, then, how I may help you."

"it is not me but an Irish- Australian flautist in our master class who is getting very worried about a teenage choir and their choir mistress…"

"a friend of his?" the sage wondered.

"Yes, we think so, Sir; he may have told your friend, our Dean, a bit more than we know, so far; he is a good person and a very good musician…"

"which is why you offered to ring me this early in the morning, my boy."

"yes, my respected teacher.."

"laying it on, Son; I tell you what; I shall ring my friend, as you rightly say, your Dean, later today; what time- your time- would be a good time, do you think?"

"mid-afternoon your time, Sir, say the third prayer; our dean starts work quite early our time."

That was what the old scholar did, having gone to the studio and then left his team and his students a bit earlier than normal, promising that he'd be back later that afternoon.

"Do you want us to pick you up later?" asked one of his students who had saved up for a battered Fiat.

"No, I shall walk…"

"I think Professor Esek does not want to ruin his hearing inside your rattletrap," the studio technicians teased the boy.

Having gone home, he got one of the girls who had just arrived from school to prepare a glass of tea, without sugar, but with a bit of lemon rind in it; he then leisurely rang his friend's number at the Juillard. The Dean was not altogether surprised:

"I am Brendan's direct supervisor and promised to help him…"

"if I understood my student rightly, a friend of your Brendan's got herself and her choir detained in Istanbul.."

The Dean explained as much as he knew.

"we need some first- hand input from somebody," the scholar committed,

"preferably here in Istanbul; what else needs to be dealt with, my friend?"

"rehearsals; they may need to be permitted to rehearse, then find space and, possibly, a conductor, depending on how and where their choir mistress is being held.."

"what is so special about the choir, other than being Australia's official choice for their age group?"

"the choir mistress is Armenian- descended, as are many of her choristers, the rest are of Kurdish Georgian, Arabic and Turkish stock, the grandchildren, as a rule, of migrants who left for Australia some fifty years ago if not earlier…"

"I can see that rub my contemporaries here the wrong way; we live under a very nationalist government.."

"do you get to notice?"

"as a Sephardi? Yes, manageably so, my friend," the musician replied: "You would like me to find out what has happened to them, and why, and get somewhere they can rehearse for the big event which is what they came for…"

"can you, Yishak?" asked the dean.

"The last bit, yes, as soon as I can locate them; the first, find out what, or who, got them into that situation…"

"do you have Armenian Kurdish or Assyrian militae and people prepared to sympathise with them in Turkey?"

"yes, we definitely have militiae, definitely Kurds, and nowadays, even Assyrian and Armenian ones, ever since their old churches in Syria or Iraq got destroyed and their co-religionists killed, imprisoned or dispersed," the old sage replied.

"even if that were not so, it'd be a good enough excuse for our present government to act, using the very suspicion .."

"how about the police and the judiciary?"

"the police do as they are told, without necessarily investigating in right earnest.."

"how about the judiciary?"

"the prosecutors lost a lot of any independence they may have had, with some very recent legislation being passed, and cases of abetting terrorism might not make it to court these days; no help from Australia or from their consul?"

"it appears not," agreed the dean,

"blame inertia, unwillingness to offend a major ally and trading partner and then add the very suspicion of aiding terrorists, my friend.."

"it is as I thought," said the scholar. "That may have to depend on the parents and sponsors of the choir- critical mass, it is called, I think; what I can and shall do is get hold of whoever holds them, likely in different places, and organize permission for them to rehearse.."

"do you know where to start?"

"yes, through our FM radio, my friend; thank you for explaining all this to me; if young Brendan wants to talk to me, let him do that also. He must be very worried for his friend."

∾

Yishak was true to his word. He told the studio manager a fable.

"when I was younger, my grandfather would take me across to Bulgaria to shoot bear; he'd buy a goat from some poor villagers, then tie it up and wait nearby ."

"is that what you call bear- baiting, Uncle Yizhak?" asked the young Sephardi.

"not exactly, that is worse; you do that to tease a tethered bear for some circus trick," answered his teacher: "but you are right, in a sense; I may need this FM radio to 'bait a bear'?"

"one of our would- be censors?" the boy asked, alert.

"Yes; now I do not know which one; what do you suggest, son?"

"I do need to know what you want to bait him with?"

So Yishak explained about the detained choir.

"We have links to FM stations in Australia, ethnic as well as mainstream ones; I can prepare tapes in Greek"

(their cither player was from a family originally from Smyrna nowadays Izmir, distant relatives of the late Onassis, people who had been permitted to reside in Istanbul after the civil war of the Twenties)

"Turkish; I might even manage Georgian through an ex- girlfriend; Kurdish I do not know," the studio manager continued, "and can, and shall, threaten to, forward these to my contacts all over Australia. Imagine our 'bear' having a heart attack if a Greek FM gets hold of that one;"

"meanwhile, you suggest that I indicate to whoever our 'bear' is that we might play our own version.."

"which they'll threaten to block.."

"which will lead to yet another set of demonstrations.."

"which they'll have to deal with in their own usual brutal way but nonetheless.."

"more bad copy overseas, as well as among the opposition,.."

"unless.."

"unless they allow the young people to rehearse and members of our team to contact, perhaps even conduct them, seeing that we are all musicians at heart."

"so tell me how to get in touch with our choice 'bear '?"

"it is usually the other way around but, it so happens, one of our singers, Uncle, used to go to school with the sister of one Kerem.."

"him the Bear?"

"no, not at all; very decent, very open-minded; he often squires his sister, I am told, as her husband is usually overseas; she married early, even by our earlier standards, and Leila visits her quite often…"

"so she knows this Kerem well enough.."

"to try, anyway, to find out whom you need to contact, Uncle. Meanwhile, I shall prepare a recording…"

"would it help if I got to interview the Australian flautist, the friend of that Armenian choir mistress, in New York, or his brother, the music teacher, in Adelaide?"

"via skype, you mean, Uncle?"

"yes, for authenticity, I'd say."

∾

Leila had not studied under EsakEbed, but revered him, nonetheless, as did the entire team, ensured that, the next time she visited her friend, Kerem would be around as well . The girls watched the children play with their computer and entertained good-looking Kerem as best they could, while his sister excused herself, ostensibly to give Leila a chance to flirt with him, if she so wanted. The girl asked him whom to contact if the radio station wanted to clear an item with the intelligence censor. This was the first that Kerem had heard about the Australian choir and its detention:

"Look, I know there are all kinds of militia operating in the border area if not in Syria let alone Iraq and we have any number of people arriving here to help them but this does sound a bit far- fetched. I can tell your studio manager whom to contact; moreover, there are Australian Federal Police stationed at the

Australian consulate; I may be able to ask them, or find out how to do it, and then tell you next time I see you here at my sister's."

∾

Early the next morning, Yishak phoned the police officer at his home:

"You do not know me, except perhaps by reputation, Colonel," the scholar introduced himself.

"I definitely know your studio; we had to close it several times, as you know, but the younger people in my family quite like your music, as do my own officers, and I do know your reputation. What can I do for you?"

The scholar explained.

"So you are baiting me with a recording that, if broadcast, would lead us to shut your studio down once again, only for it to be played all over the ether in Australia; your young people also promise to demonstrate, once again, for people overseas to take notice and for others to join, who knows? And you, Efendi, are prepared to demean your own reputation as a scholar; what for, my friend?"

"so that a choir made up of teenagers who are supposed to be our guests and to represent Australia may rehearse with my students, rather than being kept incommunicado and unable to practice.."

"they won't be allowed to sing at Chanukkalle in four days from now."

"aren't you risking a diplomatic incident of some proportions, Colonel?"

"I did not order their detention but I do admit that their parents are giving us little peace, nor are their, what do you call them.. multicultural associations."

"what do you expect, Sir? If your own children or nieces were detained in Australia and accused as these young people are, would you not do something about it?"

"so you want someone in your team to meet-and work with-the choir.."

"in return for not broadcasting their situation just yet…"

"they were split up, boys and girls; how they were ever invited to come here: Voices of the Levant.." the police officer's own voice trailed off.

"We used to live in an empire that accommodated these voices, and moreover, Colonel ," the scholar reminded him,

"we all like to watch The Magnificent Century and that's precisely what it was, a realm which had Greeks, Jews, Yazidis, Turkmen, Circassian, Armenians Arabs, Berber, Moors, Copts, Sciptars, Bulgars, Kurds, Serbs, even Hungarians, peacefully with one another. We are told to remember those glorious days but we are not allowed to act them out, are we?"

"who can?" asked the police officer.

"The Australian nation, it seems."

"so what does your radio station want, in return for not starting yet another demonstration?"

"Not my station," the scholar sighed, "but I admit to my students being among them. Yes, the idea is that each of these groups has one of my students rehearse with them for two hours every day; it won't be the same young people each time, as you can imagine."

"let me make up my mind," promised the police officer.

"Why, however, have the Australians not come up with an idea like that?"

"give them time," the scholar asserted. "If they, too, were not as blindsided by the terrorism charge as we are, they would have acted more forcefully. Don't forget that the parents cannot be threatened indefinitely.."

∾

The boys and girls had, indeed, been kept apart. Since, however, there had been several demonstration all over Istanbul, due to the unfortunate death of fifteen-year-old Erven who had been run over by a police car that had sped to break up a workers' protest, several hundred young people had been rounded up and incarcerated inside a complex normally used by the military police, the girls inside their gymnasium, the boys inside a huge hangar. Conditions inside either one of these soon began to disgrace a refugee camp.

The choir consisted of fifteen girls and eleven boys; the girls, six Turks, three Armenians, six Arabs, the boys featuring an Iraqui Kurd, two Anglos, one part-Irish, the other Geordie, had instinctively stuck to one another; things came to a head when some of the kids that had been swept up by the police had rounded up on one of the Armenian girls, with no one seemingly prepared to stop them. The choristers, however, did.

One of them, fourteen-year old Samira, Syrian, stepped in and fronted the rowdiest girls who sounded ready to lynch her and her Armenian friend.

A Turkish girl, Nadiyeh, started looking for a warden; eventually she found Aysha, a policewoman who was, obviously, stretched to her limit and did not look inclined to intervene.

"Look, we do not know why we are here and not in some hotel or school rehearsing,"Nadiyeh began,

"and these kids here are not our enemies, nor we are theirs. The Australian government selected us to sing at the Canukkalle centenary, not to fight you people.

Eventually, our parents will get here and, while you can detain us, doing it to fifty ordinary adult Australians will be a bit more difficult.

Meanwhile, we Turkish girls from Australia will defend our Armenian friends;

in fact, we will defend each other; some of us have had taekwondo, karate, judo training. You have a choice of everyone fighting everyone else,"Nadiyeh continued, "or we girls do music and those who want to can get training in…"

"unarmed combat? You must be mad !" exclaimed the young policewoman.

"Not worse than those who brought us here in the first place. Have you got a whistle, Miss?"

Several whistles were procured and in the break in proceedings thus caused, Birke spoke up, echoing her friend:

"Look, we girls were sent by the Australian government to sing at Chanukkalle, not fight you here; that was a hundred years ago. I do not know why you are here, or we, for that matter; we will defend one another if you want to pick on us, but that makes no sense to me. We need to practice, and Nadiye here will conduct those of you who want to sing; if you do not know the words, make them up or imitate the sounds; we need to practice key, tempo and delivery, not the lyrics.

My friends and myself will train those who may not want to rehearse, in either Kendo, Aikido, Taekwondo, Karate of Jiu Jitsu. Would you like to know why some of us girls know Unarmed Combat? Our parents back in Adelaide made us practice so we girls could go out day and night by ourselves; for Adelaide is no safer at night than Istanbul."

Gasps, then a horde of kids straining to get themselves in line

"We need mattresses," whispered Nadiye to Aysha:

"We'll use blankets, instead," suggested the young woman. "organize some of your girls and help us carry a few stacks of blankets inside; we'll need them tonight, in any case." So it was done.

∽

The boys had been confronted with a similar situation; as soon as some of the Istanbuli kids realized that there were Armenians (five) and Kurds (two) among the choristers, unequally balanced by one Anglo-Welsh to be precise- and only two Turks, they felt they had enough of an excuse to bully the newcomers.

Nasredddin the biggest boy, already a carrying bass voice, among the choristers; blocked some of the bullies while Ebed, a high tenor whose voice had only recently broken addressed the rest in Turkish:

"we were sent to represent Australia next week, not fight you here. We need to, and shall rehearse, no matter what happens; Graham here is a member of a police youth boxing team and he will coach some of you if you like. Meder, my Kurdish friend who speaks Kurdish (deep breath), Turkish and Arabic as well as English will conduct us; you may join, never mind if you don't know some of the songs."

Three military policemen had been expected to keep control of several hundred teenage boys; they appreciated this unexpected initiative.

∽

Khadijah who was meant to help the girls rehearse had been forbidden by her parents, unless accompanied by a boy from the studio; in the event, she, Hamid and Ezed went to Military Police Headquarters who knew nothing about the arrangement. It was not until they reached Yishak on Ezed's phone and he, in turn, had reached Fered at Intelligence Headquarters that the young people were let in,

"two hours maximum," they were told.

Ezed ended up with the boys who had organized themselves in different groups; those who knew the Turkish songs on offer were working on these while the Armenians practiced largely by themselves, with only a few.

Istanbuli boys sufficiently interested to participate. The wardens had organized some tarpaulins for Graham, the Welsh kid, to work with those who wanted to box, as well as some workmen's gloves,

"better than bare-knuckle," as the boys commented.

Ezed listened to and watched Meder conduct the Armenians and decided to help the larger group with their Turkish songs; theirs was a popular radio station and the boys did not object; they even began to tackle the typical Australian songs which the choir had meant to present and which the Armenian boys, Aram in particular, knew by heart.

∽

Khadijah and Hamid entered the gymnasium and found the girls practicing Far Eastern unarmed combat, those that were not singing, that is. Khadijah decided to help out with Karate while Hamid organized a dustbin for drums and whistled, to help tune those melodies which he knew.

About twenty minutes later, Nadiye interrupted what she was doing and asked:

"does anyone remember the text of what Kemal Pasha was saying about Australian soldiers having turned into sons of Turkish soil?"

Noticing that neither the policewoman, nor Hamid or Khadijah, nor any of the Istanbuli girls knew what she was talking about, she and some other choristers explained:

"we learnt in school in Australia that Kemal Ataturk was saying such words at a Gallipoli anniversary … "

"what is Gallipoli?"

"she means Chanukkalle," corrected another chorister: "our geography teacher back home attended last year's anniversary there."

The policewoman and the studio musicians looked at one another, then shrugged.

"I know whom to ask," said the policewoman, suddenly. "My cousin Kerem; he is with Intelligence and he knows where to look for such things," she commented.

∽

Kerem was, indeed, a distant cousin to Aysha, the policewoman who, when she was younger had developed a crush on her handsome, friendly and smart, if distant, relative. They were good friends, not that they saw each other very often, what with impossible working hours.

Aysha had reason to appreciate Kerem's knowledge of all kinds of subjects, not least because it had helped her bypass official channels.

She rang him while still at work, on an official line:

"you got them to physically practice and to rehearse, good girl," he commented.

"oh, the girls organized that; it was either that or a bloodbath.." she explained.

"what I was asked was to get the wording of what Kemal Pasha, our first president, was to have said about Australian soldiers in Turkish soil…"

Kerem thought for a while, chasing a half- remembered phrase.

"1934, I think," he finally told his cousin:" I'll look it up for you; what do your girls need it for, Aysha?"

"I think that they want to develop that into a song which they'd like to rehearse for the Centenary.."

"if they ever get to perform; it is good that they haven't given up on it,"

"for everyone," his cousin agreed, "themselves, the other kids, us girls who are to keep things under control.."

"with no help from above?"

"with no help from above, Kerem," his cousin confirmed.

Kerem rang a friend at the presidential archives in Ankara before he left work, leaving a number so as to be reached later that evening at his sister's. The friend rang at almost nine o' clock when Kerem was about to head home:

"I got the original wording in both Turkish and French; Kemal Pasha did not know that much English.."

"it was not the important language in those days that it is now," agreed Kerem. "Is there an authorized English translation?" he asked.

"I'll have a look tomorrow," his friend promised.

His sister had listened to Kerem's end of the conversation and demanded an explanation.

"You remember that I had asked you to accompany me to the sports fest at the kids' school tomorrow…"

"I nearly forgot,"Kerem teased his sister.

"Don't you dare, boy !" admonished his older sister. "with luck," she continued, "I'll be able to introduce you to at least one of the girls from the Australian consulate; we have several with kids at the school." which is how Kerem not only got to know Graham but also the English wording of Kemal Ataturk's dictum of reconciliation, of supreme importance for the relationship between the two nations.

∽

Yishak was almost the first person to hear about that project to honour Ataturk's ode to reconciliation.

While his urge was to compose the hymn himself, he had a brainwave, instead, and rang his friend, the Dean of Juillard's in New York, telling him.

"Would you wait a few minutes, and I'll ring you back.."

"I'll have another cup of tea and check a script.."

"ancient?"

"yes, Domen hymns."

"aren't they the Islamic equivalent of 'marranos '?"

"sort of; followers of ZwiSabbatai Levi who was forcibly converted in 1633 Common Era."

The dean rang a few minutes later: "Have you had your cup, now?"

Arsalan • 37

"Yes, thank you, my friend; what did you want to talk to me about?"

"Hold the line, please; my young master student from Adelaide wants to ask you something."

"I am all ear ."

Brendan took over the call: "You told my professor that the choir wanted to compose an ode of reconciliation based on the words by Kemal Pasha which he spoke at Gallipoli.."

"Chanukkalle"..

" in 1934."

"yes, that was what my young people told me."

"could you help us find the conductress; is she held separately?"

"yes, she is, apparently; what have you in mind?"

"She is not only a conductor but a composer; several of the songs that her choir is supposed to sing at the Centenary are hers."

∽

"ordinarily, we are required to observe civil obedience to our laws and the governments that enact them," commented George Mac Manus, addressing the assorted parents of the young choristers:

"but when laws are crafted and enforced against people – our children, in this case- while they are innocent within the purpose of such laws, then our duty lies with civil disobedience."

Stupendous applause; it took minutes for George to make himself heard:

"I ask you parents, therefore, to harangue Turkish and Australian leaders without ceasing, even though they may warn you off, even suss the police onto you. Also, make use of every single contact with the media, here and in Turkey, that you have or that we, Mara and myself, can provide. Yet," he paused, for effect and also to work out how best to put what he needed to say next:

"Ordinarily, it may be enough to simply not be guilty and rely on the assumption of innocence but not if you are accused of aiding and abetting terrorism. Now think; seeing that our children make up the officially sanctioned choir for the Gallipoli centenary and are neither terrorists, nor did they go to Turkey to help terrorists there, no matter who they may be and which cause they may serve; who has an interest in sabotaging them as a choir; why such a person would do it, where he was based and what help he would have had in Turkey itself.

I do not expect you, the parents, to even know where to start, even though you may well give it some thought; I intend to work through our sponsors and the media to give us an idea and guide us in the right direction.

You ask me why I am determined to help you? None of my students is involved; I did not start or train the choir; I did, however, suggest to Arsineh to involve herself in the competitive selection process that led the Voice of the

Levant to qualify; apart from which, I believe in the makeup of this particular choir and the redemptive role which it was meant to have at the Centenary and which, as a music educator, am determined it may yet exercise."

More applause..

"at some stage, we may be compelled to travel to Istanbul, all of us, to help our children; normally, that is not a problem," continued Brendan's brother:

"if the government won't let us, let them arrest us, for no reason other than stop us from getting our children, alleged abettors of terrorism, out of a Turkish jail. Agreed !"

They all nodded, some less enthusiastically than others.

"Most of all, we need to exercise solidarity, as we expect our sons and daughters to stand up for one another, in a situation they ought never to have been in."

Meanwhile, Birke's mother had worked herself through to Kemal himself, as the choir's major sponsor; she told him that, as far as anyone, knew, the teenagers had been detained for allegedly aiding and abetting some kind of terrorists or other..

"do you, does anything know anything more specific?"

"no, Sir, I have rung some relatives of mine, as have some other mothers, but we have yet to hear from them."

"Where is our choir mistress kept, and how?"

"we do not know, Sir."

"Has anyone been in touch with Australian authorities?" demanded the businessman.

"Yes, both through the hotline in Canberra and the Australian consulate in Istanbul."

"no success?" wondered Kemal.

"None," agreed Birle's mother: "they do not want to be involved with anything that reeks of terrorism."

"I shall do two things," promised the wealthy sponsor:

"I have contacts with the embassy in Ankara; likewise, I shall ring my relatives and, if needed, I shall fly there myself."

"haven't you been back to Turkey quite recently, Sir?" the lady asked him.

"yes, about four weeks ago, Mother of Birke."

"thanks, anyway; I felt that you ought to know, at least."

"thank you also," Kemal saluted her courteously and then hung up.

∾

He thought whom he could ring in Istanbul at this time of day; for Birke's mother had rung him early in the morning. He settled on an insomniac uncle who often got up at night, for a glass of raki or a cup of tea, to cope with sleeplessness; he'd listen to all kinds of radio programmes which it was often easier to receive at night than during the day, including Greek ones; for he liked their instrumental music.

"Effendi," he said as his call was answered, that being the term of respectful attention when they were alone; as no one was allowed to use that title any more. "how is our family?"

"it is good of you young people to remember us ancient ones; there has been little change since you were here."

"I missed Ismet who was in Germany while I was with you…"

"yet he has had unkind things to say about you."

"sorry to hear that, Effendi; I would have liked to have seen him; I am not aware I offended him; why?"

"I think your business interests and his overlap at times," his grand-uncle commented, bright as always.

"where?"

"I do not know, but he had gone to Dyarbakir almost immediately after his return, on behalf of a German client of his," his uncle surmised, "and I seem to remember that you had business there as well."

"yes, I did, or do."

"Maybe he missed out and blames you for it, Kemal. Was that why you were ringing me in the middle of the night, my boy?"

"I am not sure, Effendi: a teenage choir which I sponsored to represent

Australia for their age group at Chanukkalle has been detained instead.." and he continued to tell the old gentleman what he knew.

"Look, let me talk to one of the girls," (meaning his great- granddaughters), "I seem to remember that they are friendly with some of the FM people; they usually have their ears to the ground. Ring me later during the day, not at this ungodly hour, and I might know something."

∞

Later that day, Kemal rang the Australian trade commissioner in Ankara whom he knew well enough to contact directly. Courtesies over, he broached the subject:

"You might remember that I sponsored a choir in Adelaide to take part in the centenary.."

"at Gallipoli next week?"

"yes;. It appears the choir was detained in Istanbul, instead?"

"whatever for?"

"aiding and abetting terrorism."

"what?"

"that's what I said." "ISIS?"

"no, more likely some Kurdish Assyrian or Armenian extremist setup."

"we have these now in Turkey," the diplomat agreed, "and if the Turks suspect that, it'll be difficult for us to even contact let alone help them."

"I am a Turk myself," Kemal reminded him.

"sorry; of course. What do you suggest?"

"a brainwave, Brian. Have you got Australian Federal Police on site?"

"yes, we even have an officer stationed in Istanbul."

"Then ask someone in Intelligence to allow that officer to liaise with them, sort of semi-officially; for you do have an obligation to the kids, as Australian citizens, and a policeman might be of some help to them, face- saving exercise, at least, especially if that officer has good contacts in Istanbul."

"It is worth trying, I suppose,"

"your embassy is only hours away from a telephonic onslaught by two dozen quite distraught parents, same as the consulate; be proactive."

"thanks for letting us know; I'll have to talk it over with my colleagues, but why not? Things are getting a bit tense at the moment.."

"they always are, Brian."
"you are right, Kemal."

∞

Arsineh was one of these girls who was true to herself at all times and places; she was generous to a fault, passionate- physically and otherwise- in her loving and besotted with music. To have been isolated from her choir was the worst punishment, more awful even of having been arrested as a terrorist stooge. She was not in solitary confinement, however, yet had to cope with the kind of toilet and bathroom facilities that she had shuddered to hear her grandmother talk about, dark, smelly, congested and in need of a clean.

Several hours after her detention at the airport when she realized that nobody would enquire about, let alone release her, she found an old oil tin, a measure of soap, a shard she could use for scraping and a tap that could be turned off; she set to work cleaning the toilet slabs, typically for the Near East, the hand basins and washing bowls, not stopping at the tiles that still existed, singing to herself instinctively, almost without recognizing that she was doing it.

Two young women joined her after a while, one of whom spoke good English; it turned out that they had been detained after one of the Taksin Park demonstration, had yet to be tried and were unlikely to be released soon as they had attempted to organize a relay fast among their fellow inmates.

"I am Zeinab and she is Abeda," the English- speaking girl explained: "and you are?"

"Arsineh from Adelaide, Australia."

"isn't that an Armenian name?" Zeinab exclaimed, having listened to her friend's whispered comment.

"Yes, my great- grandparents migrated to Australia some ninety years ago.."
"after 1915?"

Arsineh knew that nobody in Turkey was allowed to mention, let alone acknowledge, the massacre of that year; this was the closest that the girl could get.

"yes, several years afterwards, after Armenia had to join the Soviet Union in 1923."

"We never learn these things in history.. "commented Zeinab, conveying a warning to Arsineh who, after all, was accused of aiding and abetting terrorist activity of a kind directed against the Turkish nation.

"You have a lovely voice, Arsineh," Zeinab translated for Abeda, trying to minimize the impact of talking to an Armenian for the first time in the girls' lives.

∾

It is often easier to sing in a foreign language than to speak it, especially for trained choristers. Arsineh, even though her Turkish was rudimentary and her Kurdish and Arabic close to nonexistent, remembered the choir's songs almost completely, word for word. Having survived ascending competitions so as to be selected would have helped; she had composed songs in straightforward English and another three in Kurdish, Arabic, Chaldean and Armenian tonality. When she, Zeinab and Abeda had finished cleaning all the toilets, sinks and washing areas, she started conducting herself, soon to be joined by several of the young women under arrest who recognized the Turkish songs. The guards listened with interest, making no move to interrupt. For the first time since her arrest, Arsineh went to sleep, having been given extra cups of tea, with some peace of mind, not aware that the next day would change her life.

∾

Graham had, eventually, been allowed to join Kerem in their attempt to locate Arsineh, and had developed a firm friendship with the young, sincere and very smart police officer. They asked for Kerem's cousin to accompany them and be temporarily relieved from guard duty at the military police compound where the Australian girls were held.

Kerem had prevailed on Fered to find out where Arsineh was kept which even this senior investigator was hard put. Eventually, he consulted a colleague of his who specialized in abductions, as to how to pursue such cases.

"Follow the trail from the airport and interview everyone involved in her interception, as if she had been abducted.." (which, of course, she had been, Fered reflected) "until someone can either tell you where she was sent or till you can eliminate where she is not likely to be, my friend."

Fered, a very busy intelligence officer, beset with meetings and in charge of several investigations at once, did devote a lot of time and effort to this search, surprising himself by his appreciation of Arsineh's dedication to her craft. Eventually, he was guided in the right direction:

"Their young choir mistress was separated almost from the start and kept worrying about her choir and where and how to find time and scope to practice," a lady sergeant told him. "Colonel Demirel took charge of her, as also of the lot whom he sent to the military police academy in Sirkesi.."

"is that where she is kept, Madame Sergeant?"

"no, Chief Inspector. You'll have to ask Colonel Demirel, Sir;" something which Fered did not want to do just yet, aware that he needed that man's permission, eventually, on behalf of Kerem and Graham.

As it happened, someone in the colonel's staff had apprehended a people smuggler, a rather rare event, whom Fered needed to interview quite legitimately. He rang that officer, mindful that his regular work could not wait:

"will you bring in Adegan, or would you like me to interview him in your office, Selim?"

"No, I'll have to shift him, anyway; I'll take him to barracks after you have talked to him."

"where is he now?"

"in a temporary detention centre set up for woman demonstrators, including that young Australian who was intercepted at the airport three days ago," his colleague explained.

"Why bunk him with those girls?"

"we had the workmen in at barracks; the colonel rang the matron of a juvenile detention centre requisitioned after the demonstrations, ordered her to take in the Australian and to find a holding cell for Adegan …"

"which she did; no doubt, one of her punishment cubbies."

"yes, with a bucket inside, emptied by a cleaner ever so rarely."

"Adegan will be pleased to be out of that one; bring him over, Selim; what is Matron's name; I can visualize her but cannot remember.."

Fered did recall his impression of a very strict but fair juvenile detention officer, capable of striking awe into the hearts of hardened criminal or military police. He found the location of her centre and a telephone number to go with it and rang. Having dealt with the customary preliminary courtesies, he told her:

"Matron; I need to interview that people smuggler in your care and Major Selim is coming to collect him …"

"he already has, Chief Inspector; depending on traffic, he should arrive quite soon. "

"Thanks, Matron; how is the Australian girl in your custody doing?"

"Well, she organized a cleanup and, since yesterday, she has been teaching and conducting the girl detainees in all manner of songs, not all of them in Turkish."

The Matron knew full well that a few of them were in Armenian and Kurdish, having served in the eastern provinces but did not know Fered well enough to admit such knowledge.

" How do you know that she is with me, Chief Inspector?"

"The Australian embassy has requested permission for an actual policeman of theirs to interview her on behalf of the consulate.."

"why, if I may ask?"

"well, they have a consular responsibility, for starters; likewise, as she is suspected, even if not yet formally charged, with aiding and abetting militias, they might want to interrogate her; for it is an offense in Australia as much as here."

"you realize that you'll have to let Colonel Demirel know who can easily refuse, Chief Inspector," the matron pointed out.

"That I realize," sighed Fered.

"I wanted to know from you what state the girl would be in before I send my colleague along with the Australian policeman and a military policewoman, my colleague's third cousin."

"Istanbul is a village, "acknowledged the matron;

"I know you have to have a lady officer with you; but why her?"

"Because Aysha is acting warden at the military police academy…?"

"is that where they are holding the choir?" the matron enquired. "The girl keeps asking.."

"not surprisingly; they are her charges, after all," commented Fered.

"I suppose," agreed the matron.

∾

"How did you even know that I am in charge of that Australian suspect, Chief Inspector?" Colonel Demirel demanded. "She is to be kept incommunicado at all times …"

"as is the choir, Colonel?"

"by implication, I should think, Chief Inspector."

"Aren't you surprised that the Australian embassy is trying to get in touch with her, and with the choir."

"It is their job, I suppose; but they normally are in no hurry when it concerns terrorists.."

"people suspected of abetting terrorism, Colonel," corrected Fered patiently.

"Same thing; what is your interest, Chief Inspector, if I may ask?" commented the colonel sarcastically.

"Our unit was approached by the metropolitan superintendent who, in turn. had been contacted by the home ministry acting on the consular request, as is their job,"Fered answered quietly. "To answer your other question, Sir; it appears that the parents in Australia are beginning to leave no stone unturned.."

"well, as is to be expected, "admitted the colonel, "even though they should have educated their young ones better than to support terrorism."

"They might be convinced of their children's innocence, for some unfathomable reason, and act accordingly,"Fered pointed out.

"If they are like the parents of some of these demonstrators," conceded the colonel. "Is there anything, or anyone, impelling you to take an interest?" wondered the colonel who was, prejudices aside, a very perceptive intelligence officer.

"I keep hearing that that young woman is not only worried about her charges but even more so where and when they will be allowed to practice. I have already given permission to some young musician from an FM station to rehearse with the boys and girls…"

"Good grief, Chief Inspector; I didn't know that you were a music lover."

"I am, but what impressed me was their dedication and that, I suppose, of their conductress, Colonel. You were asking me about my own interest, in addition to the formal approach by the consulate; have I answered your question, Sir?"

There was a pause so that Fered was afraid that the colonel had left the room without bothering to hang up on him.

"Who am I," he heard the officer say, "to prevent contact being made; let me repeat, Chief Inspector?"

"How I found out, Colonel? I am to interview a people smuggler; one of my specialist colleagues suggested that I treat the Australian girl's movements and eventual whereabouts as if I were dealing with an abduction; the rest is police procedure, Sir."

"Whom do you intend to send, Chief Inspector?"Fered told him.

∾

Kerem had managed to get permission to get Aysha to accompany them to the erstwhile juvenile detention centre, the military police academy having decided to give two girl trainees extra exposure in her place.

They stopped at a roadside teashop, there to wait for Graham who had unsuccessfully attempted to get an up- to date briefing from the consulate. He got Aysha to tell him about the choristers in her charge, not that she could tell him much about how the boys were doing, other than what her colleagues had told her:

"The girls have been rehearsing all kinds of songs, directed in groups, more or less according to language," she told the men, as translated by Kerem.

"Two of them also train our girls, those who do not want to join in the singing,"

"In what?" demanded Graham.

"Martial arts, would you believe it?"

"How about the boys? "asked the policemen.

"Likewise, from what the blokes tell me in the canteen. They got a junior boxer among them and they likewise rehearse.."

"without notes? "

"wondered Graham.

They were on their way, struggling with dense afternoon traffic. Kerem had the use of a police driver who knew every shortcut, including some that would have scared an alley cat, ruthlessly blocking off all and sundry.

Even then, they could have moved on foot almost as fast..

"and even quicker by metro," commented Aysha.

Arsineh's new friends had attempted to hide her when Matron started asking for her whereabouts; it was only when university- educated Zeinab overheard Graham, having had an Australian lecturer in Advanced English, that she was able to persuade Arsineh to emerge. The Matron made them sit in her staff room, excused herself but left an assistant to witness proceedings, an elderly woman who, nonetheless, knew some English and a bit of French. Tea was on tap, as were sunflower kernels, nuts, honey, biscuits and some cheese out of the staff fridge. As soon as Kerem had introduced himself, Graham and Aysha, Arsineh asked the Australian:

"do you know what charges I and my choir are being held in Istanbul, rather than being here to rehearse and eventually represent Australia at Gallipoli?"

"Allow me to attempt an answer, Miss Gergovian," Kerem tried, aware that he had never seen let alone talked to an Armenian before.

"You are suspected, albeit not formally charged, with aiding and abetting a subversive activity or activities, as is your choir?"

"of what nature?" wondered the choir mistress: "how ludicrous; what say you, Mr Chalmers?"

"Graham, if I may call youArsineh." the girl nodded.

"We have, so far, not even been officially informed about your detention, let alone of any charges against you and the choir."

"but none of these are true; we came here to rehearse, sing and then tour Turkey not to blow it up," commented the girl.

"Unfortunately,"Kerem began then noticed the assistant lean forward, suspecting that she was listening to every word and understanding a lot of what was going on. "Could you, Madame, find us a stenographer?" he asked courteously, yet indicating that this was no more request.

As soon as she had left, Graham surreptitiously opened the door, in case she was eavesdropping; she was nowhere to be seen, however.

"Look, Miss Gergovian," began Kerem: "once a person is apprehended under the mere suspicion of aiding and abetting terrorist organizations, we do not investigate, other than to find out, by whatever means, which groups and to what extent."

"so being entirely innocent is of no help altogether?" stated Arsineh, surprising herself how calm she was, having had her suspicion confirmed.

"Miss Gergovian, let me tell you something that I am not really allowed to divulge" (hence the Matron's assistant having been sent outside with a reasonable but time- consuming request) "but the only thing that might help is find out why you and your choir have been indicted and who by, in the first place; even then.."

"I thought that much, "stated the girl: "how do you expect me to do that?"

"who knows about you being detained?" asked Graham.

"I have no idea, Graham; can you find out?"

"well, it stretches my consular role a fair bit, in view of the particular aspersion cast on you and the choir,,,"

"but you are with the Federal Police, aren't you?"

"that is true," said Graham: "is there anything that I, or the consulate, can get you?"

"yes, my choir will need our scores; I don't know who's got them or where they are; yet they need to rehearse; the Centenary is only three days away."

"let me translate for you, Miss Gergovian, what my cousin has to say about your choir, boys and girls; you'll be very proud of them when you hear it."

So he let Aysha, the one with the once-mighty crush on him, tell Arsineh about her choir, boys and girls.

"Is someone visiting them?" she wondered.

"none from the consulate, I am afraid and sorry to say," answered Graham,

"but let my friend Kerem tell you."

"we managed to get some young musicians from an FM station to rehearse with them for two hours daily.."

"since when, Sir?"

"yesterday; they sent a boy and a girl to attend to your girls and two more boys to coach the boys.."

"who arranged it, Sir?"

"call me Kerem, please; may I call you Arsineh?"

"of course; did you?"

"to an extent, yes," admitted Kerem; "in the event, it was my superior who was contacted by their mentor, Esek Ebed."

"a very famous Sephardi musician and a father figure to the young ones at the FM station," added Graham. "as to the notes, I'll have to rely on Kerem, or can you suggest a contact in Australia."

The assistant had, meanwhile, returned with a girl who could take notes in English as well as Turkish, albeit not in shorthand. Arsineh, meanwhile, had time to think:

"My parents, to begin with, Graham, and George Mc Manus who is a music teacher in Adelaide.."

"why him?"

"for scores, and I want him to get in touch with the parents if he has not done so."

"I admit," stated Graham, thoughtfully, "that I was surprised that the parents haven't made more of a stink about their detained kids."

"they will, Graham," stated Kerem, "your government is likely to feel the same about suspected terrorists the same as ours does; sorry, Arsineh."

"you mean that parents would have been discouraged from investigating what happened to my teenage choir?" wondered Arsineh.

"yes," agreed Graham, "yet I would not be surprised if parents started arriving, alone or in a body, very soon. precisely because of the treatment they experience from the department in Canberra ".

"Back to you, Arsineh; you need the scores and you would like to make sure that your choir gets to rehearse properly, for the time being."

"yes, Graham and Kerem; I am pleased that you came to see me and that you found out where I was, in the first place."Arsineh then noticed that the girl was taking notes furiously.

"Can you ask her what she is writing about, Kerem?"

He did and was told that Matron needed a record, as she was bound to be interviewed by Colonel Demirel, at the very least.

"I had a brainwave just now," confided Kerem. "The studio is bound to have scoring software, Arsineh; given that you know those songs by heart, more or less, as, apparently do the girls.. let me ask Aysha;"

Aysha agreed, once he had translated that query for his cousin.

"She says yes, they know almost every song by heart that you rehearsed with them and seem to be able to conduct them with some precision; she is quite amazed."

"so you are saying, Kerem, "Arsineh smiled, for the first time since her detention, she reflected:

"if the studio team is able to score the hymns and songs which we are meant to perform, likewise, with luck, if they continue to work with my choir, on the strength of bespoke software?"

Kerem, good as his English was, was at a loss to understand what Arsineh was trying to get at; it was the note-taker, surprisingly enough, who was able to explain.

"It was my idea to begin with," he admitted ruefully. "Thank you," he told the young woman whose note-taking capacity he had asked for, in the first place.

"Yes, m y superior officer has a sort of reluctant understanding with their mentor, I shall run it past him; for that will make things a lot easier for you, Arsineh; do you realize that it was he who commented on your dedication to your choir."

"that is why I am here for, Kerem; what do you expect; thank you both for coming, and you, Aysha, as well.."Kerem's cousin smiled. "Would you, Aysha, convey messages to the boys and the girls in my choir: I am very proud of them; I apologise for getting them into this situation from the very bottom of my heart."

༄

Arsineh was later to reflect that this was the first time in weeks if not months that she had not been wracked by the pain of having lost Brendan to his wife's prior claims. As she had plenty of time for introspection, she first thought of Graham's easy camaraderie until she realized that it was Kerem's approach to her that was slowly warming her heart, undermined that it had been by the basic kindness of Turks in general, even in this peculiar situation that she and her fellow detainees were in.

She knew that Turks refused to acknowledge the Armenian massacres which had started at about the same time as the Gallipoli campaign, something that had coloured her views of Turks and Turkey, as it had her ancestors'. But here were Matron and her staff, basically kind people doing a job not of their choice, and Kerem who was, she knew, risking his career to help her, a total stranger.

∽

George had worked his way through the major sponsors by that time, aware that it was Kemal that had given most of his time, effort, contacts and money towards the choir's success; he had even inspired its title through a casual comment as he told George one late afternoon, seated at a verandah café on East Terrace, Adelaide:

"your brother, Arsineh and another sponsor were having a coffee, here," he remembered: "we were discussing strategy and someone, I cannot say who, asked what we ought to call the choir for the purpose of competing for Chanukkalle…"

"Gallipoli, you mean, Kemal?"

"yes, George, it's the name whereby it is known in Turkey. Well, whoever did, commented that the various ethnic songs to be performed represented the old Near and Middle East, called the Levant.."

"'Sunrise", explained George.

"yes, I understand that what it means; the East," said Kemal, "and that part of the East, as seen from Europe, was under Ottoman rule for centuries, as you know; we are bringing back what once belonged there, a mere hundred years ago, in that case."

George reminded him that, to the best of everybody's knowledge, the entire choir had been detained, including Arsineh, and, as far as he knew at the time, nobody had been able to contact any of them.

"Look, Kemal, "he repeated, "we all know that neither the kids nor Arsineh have anything to do with terrorism, not that we were told what brand…"

"definitely not ISIS, bit hard with the Kurdish and Armenian background of theirs, not that they aren't other groups operating in the area, from A to Z,"commented Kemal, "all of which are highly suspect to the Turkish government, from the tiniest to the most influential ones."

"well, someone must have dobbed them in quite effectively; can you help me work out who, with enough influence to get away with it, how and, most importantly, why…" he looked at Kemal who had gone very quiet.

"If you do not want to tell me who, if you suspect anyone you know well enough… a relative?"

"then, please, tell me why and we may be able to work out how," concluded George.

"Well, it appears that I did a relative of mine out of a contract he sought on account of a client of his…"

"did you know about that at the time?" wondered George;

"was it in Turkey?"

"yes, in the Kurdish region."

"was the loss such that your, say, cousin, wanted to take some sort of revenge; if so, how did he..a 'he'?" Kemal nodded, sadly. "know about the choir, for starters?"

"All I can think of there is that, while I was in Turkey, Birke's mother rang me with a progress report on how both the funding and the competition had gone," reasoned Kemal.

"and you would have told whatever family member of yours you were staying with," agreed George.

"Likely; all your cousin then had to do was enquire for himself, not all that difficult, as you can get most newspapers on the Net, these days. That leaves the question how, if he wanted to take that kind of revenge, ghastly though it is, he was able to get that one across the Turkish authorities?"

"in itself not difficult; they are quite paranoid."

"But he would have had to indict you, or else invent a situation to have gained that kind of knowledge," argued George.

"No one has come back to me with any kind of suspicion," admitted Kemal:

"so he must have used his imagination rather persuasively,

I realize. Leaves the question, whom he persuaded."

"and an even more important one," George reminded him: "how do we get Arsineh and the choir out of that one. We'll have to prove that that's what happened, and why, and then persuade people in authority to accept it, as they did with your cousin's ludicrous accusation; nor is there much time."

"three days, "agreed Kemal. "Look, I'll do what I can with those I know in Istanbul who might be able to influence somebody, and that won't be at the consulate, nor at the embassy in Ankara, I can tell you.

Meanwhile, canvas some journalists here and also the lady from the Multicultural Centre.."

"Mara?"

"and see what kind of action you can trigger through them. I know there is no time to lose now."

∾

The Advertiser's foreign editor had, meanwhile, not been slack, regardless of his sheer workload which covered events and developments on all continents breaking simultaneously, needing to be covered and followed up in depth, the very silence in Istanbul on the situation a powerful incentive. He knew several editors and senior journalists in that city quite well and, not having heard from them for the last few days, he decided to send out a feeler, through a blog: The Singing Terrorists which he had someone translate into Turkish.

He had a call at home:

"I am very sorry to disturb you that late, Sir," the caller apologized: "and my English is not very good.."

"no, it's quite all right," the editor replied, "I have only just got home, but how did you get my home number?"

"I rang your newsroom and, once they realized what I was ringing you about, they suggested I talk to you directly, Sir."

"where are you ringing from?"

"Istanbul; I relate to a team of musicians who perform at our FM station.."

"why haven't we heard from your colleagues before?" the editor asked, with some reason.

"I understand that my colleagues promised not to report on it, in return for being able to rehearse with that teenage choir from Adelaide.."

"the Levantine Singers?"

"that, apparently, is what they call themselves but we are not allowed to use that name, or report about them.."

"but some of your colleagues are allowed to work with them, you say?"

"yes, this would be their third day."

"why are you telling me, and how did you find out about us?"

"I am not tied by what my colleagues had to promise, other than not letting our own journalists know, "the caller explained:"I also read the blog and, forgive me, engaged in some electronic tracking so as to find out where your blog had originated; it is very funny, by the way; what is the English word?"

"would 'ludicrous 'do?"

"perhaps," admitted the caller: "I can think of a person who may be able to tell you ; he is our mentor but not, formally, a member, so he may feel free to tell you what he knows about your choir."

"and who would he be, my friend?"

"we call him Esek Ebed; he used to sing Sephardic songs and is a music scholar, quite well known overseas as well; you might find him on the Net. "

"do you know him personally?"

"yes, not all that well because I am technical staff; I know where he lives but not how to contact him," and he dictated Yishak Zwi Levi's address in Zirkeci.

∽

Late as it was, the editor hit the Net and also rang a music scholar who he knew kept even odder hours.

"I haven't seen or talked to Yishak for years," commented his contact; "I'd have to ring some contacts of my own which, given the time difference, I can still do tonight; it'd be late afternoon/ early evening in Istanbul. Am I allowed to know in which context?"

"ask him, if you can actually get hold of him, about the Voices of the Levant; he'll know," the editor explained, "but try to avoid mentioning that to any contact you may have to ring to get held of Esek Ebed's telephone number. Does he speak English, by the way?"

"yes, and also French and German, as well as Spanish.."

"that I understand if he's grown up with Ladino," the editor agreed.

∞

The foreign editor had gone to bed when the phone woke him, something that he was used to in his line of work. Groggily, he tried to focus on the time and could not; he had difficulty finding the reply button:

"Trevor Greig here," he managed.

"Are you the foreign editor of the Advertiser newspaper in Adelaide," asked a cultured, accented voice.

"I am YishakZwi Levi, ringing you from Istanbul.."

"sorry, let me try to remember," the editor apologized, trying to wake up fully.

"I need to apologize," said the music scholar, "it must be almost four in the morning, your time."

"probably," agreed the editor: "you must be ringing because of the Voices of the Levant.."

"oh, is that their name; how fitting," the scholar enthused. "Some of my disciples, you may call them, are allowed to visit and rehearse with them.."

"do you know where, Sir?"

"yes, indirectly, Mr Greig; the boys and girls are not allowed to tell me but they hinted that your teenagers are kept in a military camp just outside our city; I think on the Thracian side of things…"

"military police?" surmised Greig.

"How do you know, Mr Greig? "

"I' ve been poring over maps, both paper and Google version, ever since the story broke three days ago."

"Have you had very much material to go by?"

"not really, other than 'Adelaide Teenage Choir Detained in Unknown Location in Istanbul 'two days ago."

"did your government get in touch with you at all?"

"yes, to 'tell us off '; oh, sorry, that is an Australianism."

"Oh, I understand," the scholar replied.

"How are the kids coping, Sir?" asked the editor.

"Very well, considering the strange situation that they find themselves in; they rehearse in groups and those that do not, train other kids, boys and girls, in all kind of unarmed combat."

"are boys and girls kept separate, Sir?"

"yes, we have to send different teams to rehearse with them. "

"but on the same site, Sir?"

"yes, as far as I know, the place which we may tentatively identify as our national military police academy?"

"what makes you say that, Sir?"

"a day or so before your choir arrived, we had a massive demonstration by mainly young people after an incident that you may have heard about, a boy being hit by a police car.."

"yes, we wrote about it, based on an agency report."

"My impulse is to suspect that your teenagers were deposited there as well, because our demonstrators were carted to that place, as far as we know…"

"it makes sense, I suppose," admitted the editor.

"Are you in touch with the parents, Mr Greig?"

"not directly but I did talk to their organizer, a music teacher, Mr Mac Manus."

"I think I talked to his brother yesterday, if he is a young flautist studying at the Juillard in New York. He was very worried about the choir mistress in particular, Mr Greig."

"so are we, Sir? Is she kept at the same place?"

"not at all; but one of my girls rang me and mentioned that the young military policewoman who normally acts as one of the wardens to your girls was allowed to accompany a senior policeman of ours and one of yours to where she is kept. As soon as I find out where that is, I'll let you know, Mr Greig."

"Thank you ever so much, MrZwi Levi;" the editor meant it, too.

"Can you go back to sleep, seeing that I woke you?"

"No, Sir; I'll have an early cup of tea, some cereal, then I'll take our dog for a walk before my family gets up."

"I hope I did not wake them also," enquired the courteous scholar.

"No, thanks for being concerned and for ringing me; no, you haven't," the editor decided.

∽

Trevor Greig made a mental shortlist of people he should tell about this unexpected revelation; he remembered the lady's comment at Multicultural Affairs that a member of the embassy at Ankara was on home leave somewhere in

Australia; so he should ring him, whoever he was, to be followed by George Mc Manus; mobilizing two dozen pairs of parents might provide critical mass to get things moving and dislodge a story worth reporting from that wall of silence he had encountered so far.

∞

George Mc Manus soon found out and called yet another meeting:

"I do not know how far you have managed to organize a collective trip to Istanbul; I have and shall let you know the two most convenient alternatives. We now know where our sons and daughters are kept and I am beginning to develop the contacts that may guide me to Miss Gergorian's whereabouts, through a diplomat of ours on home leave and his colleague with the AFP."

That was quite true; for Graham, remember, had squired Kevin Baird's wife Elaine at their children's school's sports fest and one of Mara's contacts had been in Perth, attending the same funeral. It was George, in fact, who had put the foreign editor in touch with him, to be duly rewarded with inside info on the teenagers' whereabouts.

"Yeah, I did talk to Graham," Kevin Baird had told George, "and he has, since he took my wife to the sports fest, been in near- constant touch with a very helpful Turkish intelligence officer whom he met there."

He promised to keep in touch with George till his departure but also suggested that either the music teacher or the foreign editor got hold of either Graham or Kerem,

"but be aware of the awkward position that these two men are in also; for both governments are meant to be hard-line on terrorist sympathizers.."

"even if those kids and their choir mistress aren't?"

"of no interest to anyone," decided the diplomat;

"except the parents and the media, "argued George.

"Mobilise them, then, but don't quote or otherwise involve me."

∞

"we have two reasonably affordable choices," continued George, "seeing that fares have gone up with mere days to go for the centenary; Turkish Airlines, a very good airline, on a group booking, direct from Sydney; or Zagros Airways.."

"who are they?"

"I'll tell you, through code-sharing, from Brisbane to Dubai, then Erbil and Istanbul…"

"what? what? "

"let me explain the difference first, about seventeen thousand dollars in total or about six hundred and fifty dollars per couple, if every set of parents can come.."

"try to stop us," they told him,"but who are Zagros Airlines and where is Erbil?"

"Erbil," the teacher explained patiently, "is the capital of Iraqui Kurdistan and Zagros is the name of some mountains, as well as of their airline."

"How did you find these connections and why?"

"in case that Turkish Airlines refuse to extend a group discount," answered the music teacher quietly.

It turned out that no parent was prepared to stay in Adelaide, preferring to free their sons and daughters from unwarranted detention.

∾

The boys and girls were slowly getting used to their Istanbuli co-evals, especially the ones who could talk to them, either because they knew enough ,English or those who spoke or understood Turkish were nearby. They got fitter and some of the girls, at least, were beginning to lose weight without missing out on food; for the military police was not trying to starve any of their youthful charges, Turkish or otherwise.

The youngsters from the radio station were allowed to stay entire afternoons, to rehearse with them, after only the second day and, having brought their favourite instruments along, they had begun to teach some of the teenagers, Turks and Australian alike, how to play them.

The military police cadres quite appreciated the discipline and sense of purpose that both physical training and music practice engendered and let their various superior officers know accordingly. Tea breaks were used to play cards or do some simple, collective exercises out in the open; several Istanbuli girls commented that they had not been outdoors this much since their childhood when parents might have taken them to a park or sent them to some relatives in the country.

Both teams had brought laptops, with the camp's grudging permission, in order to record and score songs which they then printed at the FM studio. The notes proved popular and useful; it made it easier to focus on passages that needed work, or on gaps in the kids' collective memory; for they all knew how to sight-read.

When Aysha returned from her outing to the juvenile detention centre where Arsineh was kept, she was not allowed to tell the teenagers where their choir mistress was but felt free to encourage them that Arsineh was well and had not stopped asking about them day and night and that she was treated as humanely as was possible; no, her being Armenian was not being held against her.

∽

It was not only Arsineh whose thoughts were somehow directed from her plight and, in her case, from her prior involvement with Brendan. Kerem, too, could not get her out of his mind. She reminded him of an Armenian- Canadian actress whom he had seen, and admired, on cable television several years ago; not that he had ever been abroad but, he suspected, that having been born and raised overseas gave a person a completely different outlook on life, people and things in general. He even noticed that with his sister and her husband who were abroad as much as they spent time in Turkey; they thought, acted and argued differently from everyone else.

Yet, he also knew that being involved with an Armenian girl, and a suspected terrorist sympathizer to boot, was of not much help to his career; that he was prepared not to worry too much about. But would she want to get to know him better? He asked himself if it was mere human decency and compassion, knowing for almost certain that she was innocent, as was her entire choir, but unable to do anything about it, or was it genuine undeniable attraction? He was beginning to feel the latter, based on this one encounter 'in the flesh,' subsequent to these last few days leading up to it. He needed to remind himself that he was a busy policeman.

∽

Kemal who was beginning to understand that what had happened had something to do with his cousin's revenge, however misguided that was; what he had yet to work out was how Ismet had managed to create that suspicion this effectively in the 'right' person and how to counteract it, in order to get 'his' choir set free in time for the Centenary at Canukkalle.

He decided on several things; fly to Istanbul, either by himself or with the parents, put himself into his cousin's mindset so as to determine whom Ismet might have approached, then convince whoever that was of the true motive behind Ismet's action, which, in the absence of an unlikely confession, was bound to be difficult. Likewise, he could not ask his numerous relatives directly, in case Ismet got to hear about it and thwart him. He did know that Ismet's marriage was headed for divorce, not that uncommon in contemporary Turkey, especially among couples who had married at a traditionally young age.

Kemal came to the conclusion that Ismet might have a girlfriend or mistress in waiting; it was either such a well-connected young woman or a business partner who would have given him access to a decision-maker either in government or in the military. Not that these were necessarily two groups of people willing to see eye to eye, not since the advent of an explicitly Islamist rule versus the secular Kemalist army, yet both security-minded and 'into control' to a very nearly paranoid degree.

It turned out that Kemal was right on both counts; the vital contact was a young woman whose father was somebody in the ministry of defence and whose brother was a well-connected contractor who Ismet's clients liked to do business with. Her name was Hasinah, a tall, raven-haired, very elegant and smart girl with a lively, oval face and the most exquisite almond eyes, an outright makeup artist. She was a catalogue designer for the department of education, with a sideline for her brother, which is how she had met Ismet.

∾

Hasinah found out what she should have known about Ismet that Faithful had never been his middle name; Istanbul being a village in many ways, it so happened that she ran into the girl next on his wish list, Nafisah, a witty, sexy copy-writer for an ad agency used by the department. Nafisah went pale when she say Ismet's photo inside Hasinah's wallet:

"You can't be his wife, can you?" she asked her in a quiet moment, over a cup of tea,

"no, his mistress, but he is getting divorced."

"that I know, too, but.."

"what did he tell you?" asked Hasinah, interested.

"That I was the only one for him."

"well, his arithmetic is a bit woeful, don't you think?"

"what do you mean?"

"there are at least two of us, give or take a few more.."

"yes," the other girl sighed. "what to do?"

"take revenge, naturally?" decided Hasinah. "Do you know anything about him that could really mess him up, Nafisah?"

"No, do you?"

"yes, in fact; he was totally browned out <the Turkish term was much stronger but must not be printed> that his cousin from Australia had beaten him to a business deal in East Anatolia <Turks do not like describing that region as a Kurdish province>; I had told him about the cultural schedule for the Chanukkalle centenary.."

"what had that to do with Ismet?"

"he wanted to know whether that involved his cousin, knowing that Kerem had sponsored a youth choir.."

"and?"

"that choir won a series of competitions and was nominated as the official Australian contribution for their age group…"

"so what did Ismet do?"

"he thought it was one way to get even with his cousin if he denounced this choir as being made up of terrorist sympathizers."

"in the present climate.." suggested the girl.

"I agree," concluded Hasinah;"absolutely devastating.."

"what's to be done, then?" the girls looked at each other, thoughtfully.

"Find out who Ismet blabbered to and let his cousin know that it was him who did it," suggested Nafisah

"what would that achieve?" wondered Hasinah. "let's start with his relatives; they may be able to shame him into admitting what he has done and why."

"Okay, but do you think that the government would withdraw that charge, even if we told them what had really happened."

"no; yes, but it depends who were to tell them,"Hasinah announced.

"Anyone you have in mind, Hasinah?" asked the other girl.

"Yes, I think so," Ismet's former mistress told her: "I used to be someone else's mistress.."

"before Ismet?"

"oh yes, but it turns out that Ismet knew him."

"whom?"

"ColonelDemirel, "the girl replied.

"Oh, I know him, too,"Nafisah contributed.

"How come, girl?"

"his wife Tanju Ciller…"

"General Ciller's daughter?"

"is related to us through her cousin's marriage; so Suleiman was your onetime lover, Hasinah?"

"yes, till his wife reared up; she has political ambitions of her own, and we were getting really to enjoy each other's company too much …"

"without sex, even?"

"yes, Nafisah; we went to Kheshm once, when Suleiman had to visit Iran professionally. I flew to Kheshm and back by myself.."

"him paying?"

"no, but he gave me some lovely presents.."

"Kheshm is a place where nobody needs visa, true?"

"yes, so you get some foreigners who can't be bothered to get visa for Iran proper; and young Iranians…"

"boys and girls?"

"yes, to be out from under the Imams for a while, married or not"

"very expensive?"

"for them, perhaps; affordable for us or for most foreigners. Anyway, it was divine while it lasted," Hasinah reminisced.

"Did it last?"

"not much beyond that, to be sure."

"How do you know that 'our' Ismet knew him?"

"I admitted to him that I had been 'broken in' by an expert, so to say."

"was he jealous?" enquired Nafisah.

"No, but I wonder whether that did not give Ismet the idea to insinuate to him that his cousin's choir were made up of sympathizers with all kinds of militias or people generally not friendly to the Turkish state…"

"how come?"

"you realize that they call themselves Voices of the Levant, made up of no-no nationalities, such as Kurds, Armenians, Lebanese, Greeks, even Albanians.." "all from Australia?"

"yes, you name it."

"So Colonel Demirel, your ex- Suleiman, fell for it?"

"I would not at all be surprised."

"He would be in a position, singlehandedly, to have the choir detained…"

"complete with choir mistress who happens to be Armenian."

"So how do we convince him that he has fallen for a hoax? He can be very arrogant.."

"don't I know it," agreed Hasinah, from experience. "I could approach him, with some difficulty.."

"no, let me do it; my sister-in law is very close to Tanju; they talk almost daily."

"Would she be then able to persuade Suleiman to change his mind and remove the detention order?"

"set these young people free.."

"and also their conductor?"

"goes without saying, Hasinah.."

∞

Word had gotten through to Tanju, daughter of a once- mighty army general and now, with some reluctance, married to Suleiman Demirel, one of the most powerful if relatively unknown, man in contemporary Turkey, a military intelligence officer who kept highly irregular hours. Late that evening of the very same day; for no time was to be lost, she had stayed up, nonetheless, over several very strong cups of coffee:

"I shall need a photo of yours to recognize you in future," she informed her husband, sarcastically.

" Likewise?" he parried."you did not have to stay up for me," he assured her.

"Who else for?" she fired back "Your next girlfriend?"

"No such luck, Tanju," he assured her.

"I don't know, o almost useless one," she wondered.

"What brought that on, most delightful and favourite wife of mine?"

"a young woman who must have been talking to your ex and who is related to cousin Khedije."

"not a girlfriend of mine, I assure you."

"I agree with you, for a change," his wife conceded. "The girl wasn't claiming that, either."

"what did she contact you about; when.. today?" her husband's professional instinct taking over.

"Early evening; first she rang, then I asked her to come see me; I rang Hamid, her brother, to drive her home at about ten this evening."

"what was so interesting about her?"

"Nafisah; we met her once, at our matriarch's annual gathering last year; good-looking, in case you are interested.."

"what is her link with my ex as you call her?"

"oh, my husband is beginning to ask the right questions," his wife mocked him. "They shared a boyfriend, Ismet Inonu, distant cousin to your offsider.."

"Chief Inspector Fered?"

"married and about to be divorced…you know him?"

"he is a resource broker whom the military has used to get ordnance templates from Germany.."

"made of clay?"

"yes, Tanju," her husband nodded: "so he is involved with both Hashina and Nafisah, in which order, I wonder?"

"it seems they discovered about each other."

"when?"

"maybe today," answered his wife. "Nafisah lost no time to find a way of contacting me."

"what with?"

"another good question; I always that military intelligence constituted a contradiction in terms," she smiled, "but you may yet prove an exception, Suleiman."

"what point was she trying to make, you think?" he persisted.

"that the girls wanted to get even on Ismet.."

"understandable.."

"if you, the kettle, are prepared to call the pot black.." retorted his wife.

"How?" repeated her husband, unperturbed.

"You mean, how they wanted to take their revenge and how it involves me, or, rather you."

"does it?" he looked up: "Did the girl wanted to see you to feed me…?"

"Ismet appears to have been in the vindictiveness business himself, but on a vastly grander scale," his wife informed him, summarizing what Nafisah had told her, in addition to a few phone calls that she had made. "You may yet have to find a role for me as your background consultant; Inonu is a well-known name; I rang one of our bridge ladies who put me in touch with a younger cousin of Ismet's who told me that Ismet had lost out on a major commercial deal.."

"to whose advantage?"

"a joint cousin of theirs who is a Turkish Australian, an industrialist from Adelaide.."

"rings a bell, somehow."

"The girls are convinced, and Ismet and Kemal's cousin, Roxanna, confirmed it that Kemal had funded and promoted a choir…"

"you are not saying?" her husband groaned.

"Yes, what Ismet told you was based on his wish to get even with Kemal for doing him out of a deal."

"or else, it was this Kemal.."

"who recruited a number of teenage terrorist sympathizers, you figure? But even Ismet did not outright accuse him of that, did he?"

"no, but the information I based my action on was that they had arrived To abet Armenian Assyrian Kurdish and many other militiae.."

"teenagers and their choir mistress?"Tanju wondered.

"The girls are convinced, as are Ismet's cousins, that he smeared the choir to get even with Kemal; the fact that so many teenage militants show up on the most monstrous Facebook pages these days made it more credible to you and your team," his wife concluded.

"we need evidence or a confession," her husband decided.

"Do you have anything that you can hold over Ismet? "

"in return for an admission?" her husband averred. "well, I remember him being involved with businessmen, mainly from Germany, as well as with some quite large tourist companies."

"how about indicating to him that his clients might be detained, harassed or forbidden entry, likewise that his tourist ventures might forfeit certain permits, unless he admitted.., in return for not prosecuting him and some general face-saving arrangements; but do keep an eye on him," his wife advised him.

∾

Early next morning, Ismet was about to leave for SagrihehGokchen Airport when he was stopped and asked, with great courtesy but rather firmly, to attend to an intelligence matter, to, please, follow an unmarked car instead of continuing with his journey.

They finally arrived at the same military police academy where the Australian teenagers were held. Suleiman had, meanwhile, found out how to contact Kemal, using time difference to his advantage, and listened to what the industrialist had to say.

"I have always wondered how to find out what happened to my choir," Kemal had told him.

"This is the first time that someone has been able to tell me, Colonel Demirel.

I need to tell you that the parents are on their way, as you can imagine, and I am about to leave in a few hours, whether you or your colleagues suspect me or not."

He then told the colonel how Birke's mother, along with Mara at the multicultural centre had worked out that the young ones had been held on that particular kind of suspicion; Demirel smiled at the girl Birke's quick-witted response.

"would you do the honour of seeing me as soon as you arrive," he asked the choir's sponsor. "feel free to let someone at the Australian embassy know.. you are an Australian citizen?"

"yes, and I have already contacted our trade commissioner in Ankara.."

"a personal friend?"

"yes, likewise, an AFP officer in Istanbul; such is my concern about my choir. Where is Arsineh kept?"

"oh, the Armenian girl who is in charge.."

"she is Australian, as am I; is she kept separately, Colonel?"

"not any longer; I am shifting her to where we keep the choir."

"boys and girls, separately?"

"yes, but we have allowed them to rehearse, courtesy of a local FM station."

"did you talk to Ismet Inonu, my cousin? A common cousin of ours told me that he had been distinctly unhappy with me, for a reason which I had not been aware of at the time.."

"a business deal, it seems."

"you are well informed, Colonel."

"yes, to repeat; see me as soon as you arrive in Istanbul; do contact your Australian consular or diplomatic contacts beforehand if you feel less than safe, which I'd fully understand."

"I trust you, Sir; I'll let them know, nonetheless, as I may need their help to get my choir on site, in time.."

"in time means tomorrow evening, our time, as they are to perform at the crack of dawn…"

"not much time, Sir; I am leaving in four hours, Colonel Demirel."

∞

"What will you do if Ismet denies having had anything to do with it?" his wife had asked.

"If he sounds genuinely bewildered by the insinuation, I'll pick it up," her husband had promised.

"Sure?"

"Even you may accept," Suleiman had smiled at her,

"that my intelligence instincts are not entirely dormant; I also doubt whether Ismet Inonu is capable of the kind of acting needed to convince me of his innocence unless he happens to be…"

"otherwise?"

"I'll assume his responsibility for the hoax which he may have fed through Fered and confront him with the alternative.."

"which is?"

"preventing his business partners from arriving, let alone investing; likewise, put his tour companies on our crosshairs.."

"nice military language," his wife praised him.

∞

Ismet arrived at the man's office mid-morning, cowed but also annoyed; at minimum, he'd have to get onto a noon flight and miss a business day in Dortmund, by the time the Intercity from Dusseldorf would have arrived Suleiman Demirel, while not outright rude, was very brisk:

"Look, we know the people you deal with overseas and we have had an eye on several of those package tour agencies that you are involved with.."

"why that, Colonel?" Ismet was genuinely surprised.

"Because, until just a few weeks ago, we allowed huge numbers of potential tourists to arrive on package tours, only to disappear through our lengthy borders; likewise, people who want to leave their own country for greener pastures, have been known to depart Turkey as bulk tourists," the intelligence officer revealed, making it up as he went yet also wondering if he was not right, after all.

Ismet was very quiet, then commented:

"There must be something that you want me to say or do to avoid having these agencies, or my business partners, interfered with."

"There is: I would like you to tell me why you felt you had to tell

Chief Inspector Fered Inonu that the teenage choir from Adelaide was made up, in whole or in part, of terrorist sympathizers."

This met with stony silence.

"Did you want to get even with your cousin in Adelaide?" the intelligence officer asked.

"What do you mean?"

"I know that your client missed out on business somewhere near Diyarbarkir.."

"how?"

"do you mean, how do I know it?" asked Demirel, "or how he managed to get hold of the business, instead of you?"

"both, Colonel," explained the businessman, courteously but defiantly.

"I may keep you here indefinitely, the fate that your denunciation would have subjected the choir to. No one ever found out how you arrived at it; this is the most persuasive explanation we have so far, and I am prepared to run with it. Choice is yours, Mr Inonu."

"choice between what?"

"admit to me that you allowed us to think of the choir and its conductress as purveyors of terrorist sympathy; Allah knows there is enough of that around as it is; as soon as you do this, we'll allow you to proceed to Germany and promise not to harass any of your clients or partners or your tour agencies; failing that, all these things will happen and you will spend time here, in custody, as the choir and their young conductress were forced to, thanks to you."

"And if I know nothing of what you accused me of.."

"O no, I know that your cousin, the Chief Inspector, got that info from you; all I want you to do is admit to me, here, why you did it."

"in writing, Sir?"

"not necessarily; it will be sufficient if you can organize a series of trips or holidays for any chorister or any of their parents, not to mention their conductress, through those tour companies.."

"but I'll be away, Colonel, as soon as you let me go; how am I to do that.."

"there is the Internet; we'll know how to get in touch with you; likewise, you'll be able to arrange it from a distance…it is the least you can do for any of them…"

∽

Aysha took great delight in embracing Arsineh on their way to the military police academy with the help of the driver who knew how to really scare Istanbuli alley cats; Kerem had already found out and was on his way, arriving at the same time as the day's musical coaching team from the FM station, a boy and two girls. The boy, Ilyas, had a surprise which he did not want to divulge

"until later, Inspector; but I am looking forward to meeting their music mistress and working with her;" the two girls agreed:

"Arsineh knows very little Turkish; she speaks English and Armenian."

"music has his own language," argued Suleyka, a pretty, very soulful singer.

Kerem surprised himself and everyone else around him when he walked up to Arsineh and took her hands in his:

"this will be over soon?"

"today, Inspector?"

"we are trying to arrange transport to Chanukkalle for all of you late this afternoon, complete with Army tents so that all of you can settle down for the night and be ready at the crack of dawn, half past five our time; it will be chilly !"

Arsineh smiled at him: "may I start rehearsing now?"

"yes, Miss Gergovian.."

"Arsineh, please;"

"well, Arsineh, then, would you thank these three young people who have come to help your choir rehearse today?"

"of course, Inspector.."

"Kerem, please;"

"so, Kerem, introduce me to them, and be good enough to translate if need be."

She thanked them warmly and waited for her girls to arrive;

"the boys will take a while," Kerem explained: "but as soon as you are settled and ready to work, I'll get them."

"we have no notes; do you know where they are kept?" she turned to Kerem.

"I'll find out for you, Arsineh."

"We can do one better, miss Gergovian," interrupted Ilyas. "Some of my colleagues memorized all your songs between them, at least the tunes, because we could not always follow the words, and then recorded them into scoring software at our studio; we managed fifteen copies for each song, then our equipment broke down; if you want to, we'll copy the rest by hand."

"no," answered Arsineh, delighted." Any two of my choristers can share a set of notes; are they sorted?"

"yes, Miss."

∾

The girls' delight knew no bounds; first, they all embraced Arsineh, then. within minutes, they sorted out the notes and started singing, not even waiting for Arsineh to conduct them, what was the modern arrangement of an ancient Georgian warrior hymn. The academy staff dropped everything they were doing and went outside to listen.

Kerem took a few of them along, to organize the boys who had been detained separately, having wisely taken a few stacks of notes along.

The boys picked up the tune as they approached and were singing even before they had joined the girls, facing their music mistress for the first time in all these days. The policemen- and- women, and all other staff listened intently, as did the young people from the studio, standing next to Arsineh.

"Can we work in groups?" she asked them:

"yes," agreed Suleyka: "explain how, please," which Arsineh did.

∾

Someone had tried to ring Kerem repeatedly; it turned out to be Graham:

"Look, Kerem, the parents have arrived at AtaturkAirport, and the choir's sponsor is due tonight also."

"may I tell the boys and girls here?"

"yes, I'd say it is safe now."

"were the parents detained, then?"

"initially, yes, of course; your Colonel Demirel must have had a word with airport security."

"how did he know?"

"My embassy contacts in Ankara tell me that Colonel Demirel got to talk to Ismet Inonu's cousin in Adelaide who may well have told him what the parents intended. "

"where are they put up?"Kerem wondered.

"Courtesy of one of Ismet Inonu's associated tour agencies, called Atlas.."

"they specialize on Antiquity and Early Christianity…"

"so they are used to groups arriving at short notice.."

"one would think so," agreed Graham. "My boss in Ankara talked to Colonel Demirel who allowed it to be understood that he had made some such arrangement with Ismet Inonu.."

"in return for letting him go. "

"Kerem knew that he had been prevented from getting onto his flight earlier, through the police dispatcher.

"was he the bloke who dobbed in our choir.."

"dob-bed in, Graham?"

"o sorry, an Australianism, Kerem. He informed on them, I mean, for motives of his own; what were these?"

"do you know someone called Brendan Mc Manus, or his brother George?" asked Kerem, relying on what the musicians had told him.

"Not as a person, Kerem; the embassy people told me that George organized the parents; I expect him to have arrived with them…"

"how about his brother, Brendan, is it?"

"quite possibly due from New York.."

"oh, he is the one at the Juillard, sounds like nobility, the way these young musicians said it; they have friends studying at that place, on instrument scholarships."

"Please, organize the choir so they can go to the Hotel Marmara…"

"courtesy of Atlas Tours.."

"I see; Ismet Inonu.."

"part and parcel of making up; ask Colonel Demirel…"

"he'll tell me if he feels I need to know; thanks, Graham."

"It's my duty and you are my friend; one good thing that's happened."

"not the only one, my friend," the police man smiled, mindful of his newfound love for an Australian choir mistress, Armenian to boot.

∽

The parents' anger at their teenagers' treatment, not least at that secrecy, had not abated but was somewhat dimmed as the result of the long and tedious flight, even though Turkish Air had done itself proud; the girls were genuinely attentive, there was beer and wine even in Economy, the food, while not lavish, was served willingly, second helpings were no problem and, even though space on any flight to Istanbul was at a premium, the chief steward arranged for all parents to sit as they liked, with calm competence.

Flight Captain Cer Endevan was a distant relative of Mara's husband, she being the prime mover at the multicultural centre in Adelaide; a few quiet words had been exchanged, involving George Mc Manus, herself and her husband's cousin, five times removed. Word then wasallowed to filter through to his crew, in spite of the crowded flight and the incessant demands of most passengers. All in all, an exhaustingbut uneventful and well-orchestrated flight which left the parents on the European side of Istanbul.

∽

Graham, having rung Kerem and having been put in the picture by Kemal's contact in Ankara, made a courtesy call to Colonel Demirel:

"I need to thank you and your team for your prompt help, Colonel.."

"In all fairness, and under the circumstances, even Ismet Inono deserves some appreciation; the idea to use Atlas Tours and the Marmara Hotel was his; he had enough time before his own flight to Germany to make the necessary arrangements…"

"prompted, Sir?"

"in principle, certainly, but not this instance."

"Thanks where thanks are due, Colonel; I shall contact him on his return. Meanwhile…"

"any service I may be of, Inspector Chalmers(which was Graham's rank with the AFP)?"

"Yes, Sir, would you be able to lay on police or military transport if needed?"

"you mean, much as Atlas Tours may be prepared to help your choir, they may be stretched, bus-wise, with all and sundry heading for Chanukkalle at the same time, not mentioning breakdowns, etc.

Wise precaution, Inspector. I may be able to alert our army bases on the way, likewise with our mobile police units, to help you out, if it turns out to be absolutely essential.."

"we know the demand on your services, Colonel, at this particular time; if, however…"

"I understand, Inspector. Rest assured; moreover, I shall order your friend.."

"Inspector Kerem Behli?"

"yes, him, to follow the choir, so if anything goes wrong at this late hour…."

"thanks, Colonel Demirel."

"my compliments and my apologies to the parents; how was their flight?"

"They are coming through now; I have yet to ask them but they look as one usually does after a long flight. Did you facilitate their passage through immigration and customs, Sir?"

"Naturally, Inspector. Bye for now."

☙

Kerem took Aysha and Arsineh, as well as the three young musicians, to the hotel in his car, having arranged for two military police vans to transport the boys and girls, separately, each accompanied by uniforms, until such time that they could be handed to their parents. The choristers did not stop singing and the uniforms, by now familiar with at least some of the tunes, joined them. Traffic forced them to a standstill, as was to be expected; Bilke, resourceful as usual, asked her minder for the lend of her phone and for Aysha's number.

"Aysha," she began, "could you find out the number for Marmara Hotel and ring the reception if our parents have arrived; if so, could they ring you; if not, let them know that we are on our way.. how long will it take, you think.."

"this is worse than a typical Istanbuli traffic jam, Birke,"

Aysha told the girl;

"people are getting ready for the Centenary as well; it's going to be a long weekend. I'll ring the hotel," the policewoman said, noticing from the corner of her eye that her adored cousin's hand was touching that of the choir mistress.

Arsalan • 73

❧

The parents, too, were stuck in the same traffic jam, so Graham rang Kerem again who, reluctantly, moved his hand away from Arsineh's, to answer the call.

"Where are you, Graham?"

"on Bulevar Ataturk, some two kilometers away from the hotel. "

"we'll have to commandeer a military barge," decided Kerem; "the tunnel is clogged up and the bridges are no better."

"How's the Metro, Kerem?"

"full to overflowing, I suspect, but worth a try; how about you, Graham, anywhere near a Metro station? "

"I'll ask the driver… yes, I can see one ahead."

"ease your parents out of the buses, ask the drivers to drop their luggage as soon as they can move; it might help if the parents tipped them with whatever money they have, and then get them into the metro station; Marmara Hotel is not too far from the line; you'll have to ask for directions. We'll do the same but it will take us longer. Graham, make sure that the parents do not lose each other; if they do, tell them to ask for Hotel Marmara and get off at Drakoglu Station."

It still took an hour, even though the metro trains were running, threading the parents and the teenagers through the sheer packed masses of commuters; each lot missed several trains till they got close enough, with the Istanbulis on the platforms finally giving way to the foreigners, out of innate hospitality.

The scenes at the already- busy hotel foyer were beyond description, children in their parents' and in each other's arms, as were Keremand Arsineh, almost unnoticed by anyone.

"After this is over, my love," he whispered into her ear.

"I'll give it some thought," she assured him, gravely.

❧

Graham managed to get everyone' s attention.

"Could I ask you parents to move into whatever rooms you were given, unless you want to listen to your sons and daughters rehearse; George and Arsineh, are you ready to rehearse with them; the hotel will let us use their stateroom. George, do you know if your brother is coming?"

"yes, he texted a few hours ago; he and Monique are due during the night."

"they'll have to head straight for Chanukkalle, then. Ask the concierge for help."

∾

After rehearsal, the teenagers had joined their parents for a decent wash and some sleep, knowing that they were to leave late that evening.

"as long as you are awake, keep singing to yourselves,"Arsineh had ordered them. "and have some warm gear ready; nights can still get quite cool, and also water. Tap water is all right, if you let it run long enough.

The hotel'll give as a feed, ekmek<loaves of bread> sausage, cheese and honey; I'll organize a few thermos."

Having done this, with Kerem's, Aysha's and George's help, she and Aysha went to catch up on some sleep, having been given a twin-share.

"do you love my cousin," the policewoman asked in her halting English.

"does it look that way?" the choir mistress wondered. "Yes, it does."

"then I do," suspected the girl; "others often see these things clearer that one does oneself."

"can you take time off, after tomorrow?" Aysha enquired.

"Now that the parents are here; I suppose I can."

"make sure that Kerem can take a few days off as well and make the most of it."

"you are right, Aysha; but let me concentrate on tomorrow, it was not exactly the best preparation we had.."

"aren't you being not thank…"

"ungrateful, to the young musos, you mean?" demanded Arsineh:

"no, I appreciate what they have done and also your help, and that of many others; yet we represent Australia and .."

"you are trying to do the best job you can, Arsineh; you will; I promise,"Aysha told the other girl.

∾

They hit the road rather later than expected; for one of the tour buses had developed trouble while on its way. Traffic was massive, crawling rather slowly along the Bosporus. This time, Arsineh had mixed boys and girls, leaving Birke and Suleyka in charge of the second coach: "get them to rehearse," she told them.

The inevitable happened: the coach with Birke inside had incurable engine trouble; as soon as the girl observed the driver getting nervous, she rang Arsineh: "Miss Gergovian, our bus looks like dropping out.."

"look,Birke, give it another five minutes or so, then ring Kerem Behli; he is supposed to follow us and he may be able to arrange backup…"

"do you have his number, Miss?"

"yes.."

Birke decided to ring the inspector straight away, however:

"Inspector Behli, our bus is about to break down," she told him, in Turkish, as soon as she had explained her role.

"Birke, ask the driver to talk to me," Kerem instructed the chorister who passed her borrowed telephone to the driver.

"Yes, I suspect the head gasket; I had problems before we left, Inspector."

"would you have been able to get another coach?"

"no, not with Chanukkalle coming up, Sir."

"park the bus, then; keep the lights going and the engine running; I'll organize an army truck," mindful of the promise Graham had extracted of Suleiman Demirel.

He rang the Conolel's office, unsuccessfully, then thought of contacting Chief Inspector Fered, his immediate boss.

"leave it with me, Kerem,"Fered Inonu decided, "but give me the choir mistress' number, also the girl's who rang you in the first place; does she speak Turkish?"

"she is a Turk, albeit born in Australia, Sir."

"Good."

It took awhile for the army truck to arrive from a base close to Izmir and not all that easy to shift the teenagers onto its tray, as only very few of them had brought torches.

"Do you want to follow us?" Birke asked the bus driver, "or wait here?"

"would you leave a thermos and some food, please?" the man wondered, rather embarrassed to demand that of a mere teenager, however capable.

"you may have mine and let me organize some food, "she determined.

"Lock up your bus and go to sleep, "the army driver suggested; "have you got an eye patch? There'll be plenty of headlights."

"I'll manage, thank you, and thank you also, Birke; sing for Australia, my girl !" he added.

∞

Kerem and Graham's car arrived just as the army truck was about to leave; Graham got on, sitting next to the driver, while Kerem continued, relying on his police driver to keep them abreast of the queue.

"How about the parents, Inspector Chalmers?" asked Suleyka.

"Call me Graham, for the duration, at least," suggested the AFP officer.

"Their bus is so large that it got stuck in traffic; they will be late for the dawn service…"

"will we manage?" asked Bilke, rather calmly.

"Well, your choir mistress had the right idea, to mix you up and carry you in two separate coaches; as long as she, and they, get to Gallipoli in time, she can set it all up and start when it is time; we might have to explain your absence.."

"rather not, if we can avoid it, don't' you think?" Birke offered.

"We are in good hands,"agreed Graham. "This is obviously a good driver. Girls, please compliment him."

∞

In the event, their truck overtook the other coach and arrived at the reserved parking area and, being an army vehicle, was let through. Kerem's car had got to the barrier ahead of time but decided to wait.

"I'll remain here,"Kerem explained to Graham over the phone,

"till the coach arrives, with Arsineh's half of the choir in it."

"not to mention Arsineh herself?"

"is it that obvious, Graham?"

"yes."

∞

By the time they all arrived at their designated spot, the very first hint of dawn could be seen in the slow fading of the stars which, due to a new moon, had been very strong.

"Keep humming to yourselves, boys and girls,"

Arsineh admonished her charges one more time, then finding the best spot from where to see and conduct her entire choir, given that she'd face the rising sun by the time it was her turn.

"I shan't see you clearly," she explained:" but you can; you'll need to look at my hands and face for when I cue you in."

∽

Brendan and Monique had made it to Istanbul, to be greeted by George who kissed his sister-in-law, hugged his brother and ushered them to his hired car.

"Try to get some sleep as we drive," he advised, "it will take ages to get us to Chanukkalle.."

"eh?"

"that's what they call Gallipoli here," he explained.

"Has the choir been freed," asked Monique practically.

"Only just now, at about the time we arrived."

"how about Arsineh?"

"she, too, and well-looked after by Kerem and his cousin,"

George added, with faint yet gleeful relish.

"Who are they, for crying out loud?"

"two very helpful Turkish police, brother.."

"and already friendly with your choir mistress,"commented Monique perceptively while fetching her photographic gear.

"This twilight is something very special; what time do they start?"

"dawn is just after four, Monique," answered George.

"I understand that the trip would normally take three, max four, hours, but not tonight; you can see the traffic for yourselves."

Monique did not answer, busily taking pictures. Brendan did, however, ask George on how he had managed to organize the parents

("like herding cats?") and told him, in turn, his conversations with the old Sephardic musicologist, based on his Dean's and his fellow students' contacts.

"lovely bloke, sharp as a butcher's knife, old- world courtesy, you name it, Yishak Zwi Levi is it.." His brother agreed:

"I did not get to talk to him, but Mr Greig, the foreign editor of the Advertiser back home, did; that's how we found out not only where the kids were but also that the Sirkezi FM had been able to rehearse with them. "

"but not where Arsineh was kept? "

"no, except that she was kept separate from her choir."

"Whatever for?"

"we never found out. Kerem, his cousin and Graham, an AFP bloke stationed here, did get to see her once, so they knew how to bring her back when she was eventually released. Now, please. go to sleep; for we'll have to take turns when jetlag overtakes us. I had a bit of sleep so I am driving now."

∞

Kerem, Aysha and Arsineh arrived somewhat earlier that the first coach and Aysha turned thoughtfully aside.

"You are concentrating on your choristers and on doing right this morning," the policeman stated, holding Arsineh's hands;

"yet I want us to spend a few days together…"

"here in Turkey?" she asked: "there must be some lovely resorts."

"that wouldn't work,"Kerem stated quietly.

"Because we are not married?" she asked. She had her answer when Kerem looked at her, somewhat sadly:

"I see, because I am Armenian, even though I am Australian."

He nodded: "if you want us to, I'll think of something, Now that the parents are here, there'll be less need after this morning…"

"possibly," the girl agreed:

"I certainly want to get to know you better.."

"my love !"Kerem concluded tenderly.

∞

The army truck arrived and the kids burst out, selecting a site where they could lie down for the next few hours yet close enough to where they needed to be in the morning. Arsineh made a quick decision:

"we won't do the Kurdish and the Georgian songs just yet because those who know them best are stuck in the coach; stand up, we'll rehearse without notes; those with torches, please help out."

They sang quietly while others arrived and tried to settle down; no trace, however, of the remaining choristers.

"could you ring the coach, Kerem.."

"Cer?"

"is he out of range?"

"let's try."

Kerem got through to his junior colleague sitting in the remaining coach:

"How much longer will you be, Cer?"

"something's wrong with the engine, Inspector. Could you radio for help?"

"I shall have to, Cer," Kerem agreed and chose an army frequency to call for a backup, relying on Aysha to help Arsineh as much as possible with the choristers which she did, by sharing out food, blankets and hot tea.

"Kerem will do what he can," she told her friend: "he loves you and cares about the choir," she assured Arsineh in by now surprisingly confident English. The choir mistress gripped her hand in agreement:

"I know he's risked his career; so did you; you are both good people, and I love him, too," she added, almost as an afterthought.

∾

Kerem had not stopped giving out his mayday call on both army and police frequencies, stating the location and the registration number of stranded Atlas coach. Eventually, he got a truckie to answer who told him that he had gotten on police frequency

"by mistake, Inspector; how can I help?"

Kerem took a deep breath and decided:

"look, thank you for starters; this is Cer's mobile number; ask him if the coach is on radio; then try and raise some of your fellow truckies, see if they can pick up our choristers; we have thirteen waiting, boys and girls, ages thirteen to sixteen…"

"where are their parents, Inspector," the truckie asked sensibly.

"Stuck in traffic, as we got out of the city."

"stands to reason; I wouldn't have left Town if I hadn't have to; I can pick up four unless I get charged for carrying passengers ."

"no, I'll settle that if it comes to that, my friend; will you raise another two lorries and drop the young ones as close as they'll let you to Chanukkalle; we can send our army truck to pick them up. Let me know, please, whatever you do."

"certainly, Inspector."

Kerem went over to Arsineh and reached out with his free hand.

"Any luck, my love?" she asked, quite anxiously. He told her.

"You need to stay on air, then, Kerem," she agreed, leaning against him for a few moments:

"Aysha and I can manage with the young ones; they are so tired, as you can hear.." their regular breathing could be heard wherever the young ones had slumped to the ground.

"To be that young and sleep wherever you are.."

"do not forget, they were incarcerated and now they are free, as am I, thanks also to you; that has a lot to do whether you can sleep like a baby or not."

∾

It was still dark, with the faintest hint of dawn, visible only if you knew your way outdoors, and Kerem must have fallen asleep; the radio might have run out of batteries; for it was a ringtone that woke him.

It took him a while to register:

"Chief Inspector Fered Inono gave us your number, Inspector, to be on the safe side."

"thank you, Sentry," Kerem managed: "what do you need to tell me?"

"two lorries have arrived but they are not allowed any further…"

"do they want to, Sentry?"

"no, the last thing, with cars and buses simply piled up here."

"do they want to drop several Australian teenagers where you are?"

"yes, that seems to be the idea, but one of the drivers says there was yet another lorry on its way, with five kids inside, Inspector."

"that is likely to be the case, sentry; thank the drivers and let them go, then wait for the last lorry and let us know when it gets here.." and he explained what he had arranged.

∾

It was now getting very close to dawn and Arsineh and Aysha were starting to wake up the sleeping kids and beginning to arrange them in position.

Kerem waved to Aysha who raced to see what he wanted: "you are a good girl," he praised his cousin. "I managed to get a few truckies to pick up our wayward kids, we are waiting for one more, then we'll have them here. Could you stay near the radio and hang on to my phone, in case the Sentry rings again; I'll wake the driver and get him to warm up the truck before Arsineh starts a last-minute rehearsal, so he can dash off as soon as I get news."

He kissed her forehead and strode off, knocking against the window on the driver's side which the man had wound up to protect himself from the chill air. The driver opened the door, barely awake.

"start the engine and be ready to drive off to the security gate as soon as I give the signal; the young ones are being dropped there; we are waiting for one more group of five; once you have picked them up, drive as quicklyas you safely can.."

"should not be too many vehicles between Chanukkalle and here, none allowed to," the army driver commented. The radio blared into life.

"This is Sergeant Dras, Inspector. A bus has just arrived at the security gate, full of a group of adult Australians and some kids; some of them speak Turkish.."

"They are Turks, albeit from Australia, Sergeant."

"Us Turks must be everywhere, for sure, Inspector. All my family is in Germany."

"are they the parents of our choristers, Sergeant?"

"it seems so, and they must have picked up some of their own kids on the way; it looks as if they arrived at the wrecked coach the same time as a truck did, ready to pick them up."

"how do you know, Sergeant?"

"we follow radio traffic, including civilian two-way, Inspector."

"why, then, did your unit not respond when I first called out?"

"I knew you'd ask that, Inspector; we had no transport to offer. What do you want us to do?"

"are the remaining teenagers with you, Sergeant?"

"yes, at the sentries' where the previous lorries had deposited them.

We had a job helping them turn around."

"thank you and your men, Sergeant, including the sentries; please, put them on the bus and allow the bus through."

"I'll do one better. I'll send a sentry on his motorbike to guide them through all the roadblocks.."

"of which they'll be many. "

"you are not wrong, Inspector."

∽

The bus burst through the sparse countryside in the slowly emerging dawn, coming to a screeching stop in front of some rather amazed spectators, Australian, New Zealanders and Turks, spewing out parents and teenagers alike; Arsineh sent Birke and Aysha to gather the remaining choristers and hurry them so that she could start; for the dawn was fully on and they were running a few minutes late in what was meant to be a perfectly choreographed parade; no time for any introductory speech, however brief.

Graham, Ayesha and Kerem took up position by her side, with Graham waving a mysterious folder, similar to the ones the choristers were holding.

Kerem leant back and breathed deeply, giving a signal to the teenagers to do likewise; they stretched and stood tall, tired and unwashed that they all were, all eyes on their conductress

Arsineh exhaled, then raised and brought down her left hand, unable to read her score and so placed that she could not hear any voice, directing a tune which she had had little time and opportunity to work through, other than in the hotel and on their drive.

The choir did not miss a cue and hit every single note, clearly and crisply in the morning air, as it was slowly getting light, the sun rising beyond the horizon causing a slow breeze.

Most in the audience were unable to understand the Armenian songs, even though they appreciated their liturgical echoes; people smiled and tapped their feet at the martial nature of Kurdish chants and allowed themselves to be enchanted by the lilt of Lebanese hymns of bereavement and utterly bewildered by sonorous Aramaic psalmistry.

Crystal-clear soprani soared into the slowly opening sky, undergirded by purposeful yet gentle, melodious alti and strengthened by the occasional bass among the boys; Birke and Cer, two young Australian Turks, sang a duet featuring parents' lament of their fallen son while Suleyka and Samira, two Syrian and Lebanese Arab girls, recited the breathless, joyful surprise of girls finding their lovers or brothers alive after many years.

Meder and Leila, two young Kurds, sang about a young man choosing the heroic life and a girl encouraging her lover in his chosen course, much as her heart would break.

An Armenian and an Assyrian kid sang responsive liturgies in memory of the fallen, like the Kaddish, the Jewish prayer to commemorate the dead.

Arsineh stepped forward and sang a song written by Komitas, subsequent to World War One, expressing the randomness of survival, in Armenian, to be upstaged by Kerem and Aysha intoning Kemal Pasha's 1934 speech about the soil of Turkey and the mothers of Australia, secretly scored by Yishak Zwi Levi and the FM musicians.

∞

The ultimate surprise was offered by Graham, introducing himself and his contribution in a few well- chosen words in both Turkish and English; he then offered his carefully concealed score to Arsineh:

"Miss Gergovian, are you game to sing the English version with me?

This is the score, also by Esak Ebed, or Yishak the Sephardi, in English instead of Turkish."

Arsineh took a quick look, nodded, then hummed the first notes, allowing Graham's baritone to sing the first line aloud; she then joined, a strong, utterly haunting mezzo-soprano, facing the sun as it finally rose above the Anatolian horizon.

∞

The island of Kheshm in the Persian Gulf is one place where you may observe both sunrise and sunset above the waters from one spot, if you like; both times of the day are equally spectacular, colouring the waves as much as tinting the coastlines in shades ranging from ochre to a steely pink, in the evening, striking the same tones in the morning in reverse.

Kerem and Arsineh could not get to see enough of it, given that temperatures had yet to reach the stratospheric levels typical of the Gulf in mid-summer; there was a faint but invigorating breeze in the morning and a softening of the heat in the afternoon. Neither of them would have ever thought of spending precious days on an island that belonged to the Islamic Republic of Iran, had it not been for Colonel Demirel:

"would you like some days off, Inspector?" he had asked Kerem while still at Gallipoli.

"Yes, thank you very much, Colonel."

"would you like me to make a few suggestions, Kerem?"

"Sir? "

"here they are: first, take the girl along with you, second, avoid Turkish resorts, you know why; head for Khesh, instead."

Kerem's reply expressed his bewilderment:

"Isn't that off the Persian coast, Sir?"

"and what is so special about it, you may ask. Let me tell you; it is a kind of escape or safety valve for young Iranians, at those who can afford to stay there for a few days.."

"no restrictions, very few questions asked.." Kerem was beginning to understand.

"even less so for foreigners; even being of Armenian descent, a no-no in this country, does not matter at all."

"no dress restrictions on women, Sir?"

"observed in the breach if at all; don't expect bikinis, mind you, but exposure to the sun is all right. Young Iranian women get away with quite a lot even in Iran itself; Khesh is more like Dubai if you have been there."

"yes, Sir; will Miss Gergovian need a visa?"

"not to my knowledge if you arrive from Istanbul, Kuwait or Dubai; if you want to take her to Iran proper, your hotel can arrange that."

He had then proceeded to pass on the address of the hostel where he had parked Hashina, omitting to mention her existence, let alone her role in that brief but very enjoyable stay of theirs a year ago.

The concierge had more or less confirmed what Colonel Demirel had indicated; the fact that they were not married had not entered anyone's consideration and:

"if you want to go to Isfahan and Shiraz, I'd be happy to recommend the many Armenian churches in Isfahan and there is also one in Shiraz which has the most beautiful rose gardens in full blossom at the moment; two of the most beautiful cities not just in Iran but in the entire Middle East."

"how about a visa for Miss Gergovian?" Kerem has asked.

"None for you, as you know, I can arrange a visa number for Miss Gergovian within the day which she can then take to the visa office; alternatively, you pay for a visa on arrival, especially if you want to continue to Dubai, Abu Dhabi or Bahrain on your way to Australia;

I can arrange the connecting tickets…"

"rather than having to return to Istanbul.."

"it would give us an extra day and be a wonderful experience," Arsineh agreed,

"yet I would also like to spend time here, doing very little."

"highly understandable," commented the hotel clerk. "make up your mind at your own speed."

"would I have to dress up in Iran proper?" she wondered.

"No more than what most of our own young women get away with, a hijab showing a bit of hair and anything that covers your arms to your elbows and your legs to somewhere below your knees, loose-hanging trousers are okay," the clerk commented.

"Some of the girls in my family compete with each other how to show more hair than hijab; they wear it down almost to their ears."

Kerem and Arsineh smiled at each other, replete with memories of delightful days and unforgettable love nights.

Milton Keynes UK
Ingram Content Group UK Ltd.
UKHW050747210324
439796UK00015B/1360